Ignore The Voices In Your Head

Ignore The Voices In Your Head

Julius Kane

Maverick Media Grou

For My Family

Ignore The Voices in Your Head

Julius Kane

Maverick Media Group

First Edition First Printing
Ignore The Voices In Your Head

Contents

Rescued

They said last summer was the hottest on record. Animals left outside were dying and the New York City concrete was damn near melting people's tennis shoes. There were no trees to take cover and if you found one, there was already someone else standing underneath it. But today was hotter than that. The sun seemed to come out earlier each morning, which means as soon as I went outside, I started sweating. There's nothing worse than going to work wet and sweaty. In fact, it's downright embarrassing. That's why I always take an extra shirt along. It usually comes in handy on days like this. My boss was fussy, angry, and obnoxious. I guess he was a product of his dog- eat- dog environment. He liked us to look clean-cut and professional in case one of our prestigious clients happened to drop by.

I was a mid-level advertising executive. That simply meant I made enough money to live in New York without having a bunch of annoying roommates. However, I couldn't afford medical insurance, a dog, or a real girlfriend; at least not one that was worth having. So, I went out with bar flies, heavy drinkers, pole dancers and college girls; dropouts who spent their nights trying to find themselves. I was probably the most predictable 25-year-old in Manhattan; go to work...go to the bar...try to get laid...go home. But yesterday, Lauren Tisdale smiled at me while getting off the elevator. And that was the highlight of my week.

I waved back; casually. But inside I was super excited. By inside I mean, inside my pants. Lauren Tisdale was a top-level ad executive with a body that could bring an impotent man back to life. She had the figure of a Tik-Tok model with a million followers, if you can understand that analogy. She dressed smart and sexy but not too revealing. Every guy in the building wanted her. She was a real head turner. They all salivated like wolves whenever she was around. She was out of my league, so I figured why bother? She never noticed me before. No matter how often I stared at her magnificent backside, every time she passed my cubicle, she never looked in my direction. But yesterday for some reason, I caught her glare.

After work, I go two blocks over to Johnny Ray's Bistro. They had reasonably priced hot wings and happy hour beer. I'd been going there so long I practically had my own table. It didn't hurt having the owner as a friend, either. That's where I pick up those drunk barflies I mentioned. I left the bistro about 9:30pm. I had a nice buzz and a drunk 5'2" cougar on my arm. It was a short 15-minute walk to my building. But I decided to take a shortcut. What the hell? I wanted to get Darby, Margie or whatever her name was, back to my place before she could get sober. Women were always more lucid and freakier when plied with enough alcohol.

"Cute guy like you, doesn't have a little woman at home?" She hugged my waist as if we were a couple.

"No, I work too much. I don't have the energy for anything serious, you know," I sort of chuckled. My fake laugh jumped out whenever I was forced to engage in small talk.

"It ain't all it's cracked up to be. My husband's been cheating on me for months with my son's math teacher, Miss Crumble. She sounds like a real bitch... Crumble!" She repeated the name laughing. "And I saw their text messages, disgusting! But I'm not worried. All the things he did with her I'm going to do with you. Two can play that game," she squeezed my butt.

"Well then let's play that game!" My immediate erection-that I call **Stiff John** agreed. Sure, I gave my dick a name. A lot of guys do.

"Oh, you're so cute!" She moved in close. Her breath smelled like stale draft beer.

She squeezed my butt again. I smiled awkwardly looking around to make sure her husband wasn't following her. The 5'2" woman was clearly older than me. She was fairly attractive in a construction worker kind of way. Then again, after enough beers, most women become fairly attractive.

We were about a block away from my apartment when we heard the woeful cries of a cat. Yes, a feline alley cat crying; meowing and meowing. It was awful. "It's coming from that dumpster." My soon to be one-night stand pointed and begin walking towards it.

"We don't have to go see what it is," I laughed, but was dead serious.

"That poor cat. It must be hurt," she said softly. "And what are you, some kind of animal hater?"

"No... no, of course not, Margie I just..."

"It's Mandy. Like the song. And let's help the little quitter," she insisted.

The thought of not getting laid because I seemed inhumane to animals forced me and **Stiff John** to follow her over to a nasty, smelly dumpster. Yeah, the little head was doing all the thinking.

"Oh look, it's two cats!" The drunken woman frowned. "And one of them isn't moving," she said.

It was two cats all right. One was a big, hairy, black cat with unusual red eyes. He creeped me the fuck out immediately. The other cat was white, with a black spot on the side. It was obviously dead.

"Somebody threw these poor cats into this dumpster. And one of them died. Poor thing. Quick, give me your jacket," she ordered.

"Huh!" I frowned.

"We're going to rescue this cat and take it to an animal shelter in the morning," Mandy smiled like a true good Samaritan. "This black one's a boy." The animal allowed her to pick it up without any resistance.

'Jesus Christ!" I mumbled. The thought of putting my work blazer around some feral cat, this drunk bitch was taking out of a filthy dumpster, made me cringe. I realized she wasn't just intoxicated; she was probably a little crazy too. Reluctantly, **Stiff John** forced me to hand over my blazer. I quickly changed the subject so that I wouldn't think about how desperate I was. "Hey Mindy, you never said what you did for a living."

"Well handsome, I'm a forklift driver at the new Amazon warehouse. Yeah, I'm good at working gears, real good." She let out a drunken laugh accompanied by more booze breath.

We covered the big cat with my jacket; me, a little drunk and her, more drunk. I stayed calm but still, a man gets a relieving kind of excitement when he knows he's going to get laid at the end of the night.

Another Dead Cat

As soon as I got home, I poured some milk into a bowl and set it under the kitchen table. I was hoping my kindness would show Mandy my humanity and we could move faster into the main event.

"See, you're a sweetie," she smiled. "Where's your bathroom?" She kissed me while trying to pry her tongue into my mouth. But I wouldn't part my lips. I could only imagine where her mouth had been.

Once she shut the bathroom door, I rushed into my bedroom to make sure I still had condoms. *Oh yeah!* I grinned, and fist pumped like I'd just hit the lottery. As I took my clothes off, I glanced down the hallway and saw the hairball I had rescued, had turned the bowl of milk over on my new carpet.

"Jesus Christ!" I knew this was a bad idea. I rushed into the kitchen to clean up the mess. "So, you're a finicky cat, huh?" Mandy emerged from the bathroom butterball naked. She posed in the doorway like she was some kind of 1950s movie star. The old, truck driver looking woman didn't have a bad body though. I was surprised at how perky her breasts were. I was so anxious and horny I almost jumped out of my boxers.

I took her hand, leading her into the bedroom. She was kissing me, rubbing all over my body. I loved it too. And once again I happened to look up and there was that dirty, hairy cat staring at us; just watching. It was weird. It was eerie. "There's that cat again," I mumbled. I stared back at the intrusion.

"Forget that cat! Missy is going to have her way with you?" She sounded like a hungry woman walking into a buffet.

I took a deep breath and tried to re-focus. "Lie down baby, **Stiff John** is waiting for you," I whispered. "Wait a sec." I shut and locked the bedroom door. I kept thinking that grungy cat may come into the room and scratch me while I was in mid-stroke.

Five minutes later Mandy snatched the door back open. She was cursing.

"You selfish bastard! I could've gone home and got better than that. unbelievable!" She slammed the bathroom door. She was angry because of my premature ejaculation.

The trash-can cat was now sitting right outside my bedroom door, leering, almost smirking. In fact, I had to step over it as I pretended to beg Mandy not to leave.

"Just give me a few minutes and I'll be ready to go again." I knocked at the bathroom door. That's when I heard laughing. Not a deep laugh but you know, a satisfying snicker.

"Wait! Wait!" I stopped Mandy midway between her vulgarities. "Did you hear that? Who's that laughing?" I looked around the apartment. Goddamn! Did her husband follow me home?

"What?" She huffed. "Oh, stop it! Don't tell me that on top of being a minute man you're a fucking whack job." She hurried to put her clothes back on. She grabbed her raggedy pocketbook and headed for the front door. "And don't even think about calling me." She rolled her eyes and lit a cigarette.

"Actually, you kind-of didn't give me your number," I shrugged. And there it was again, laughter. It sounded like some guy was nearby listening to our conversation. I moved her out of the way and snatched open my front door. I thought maybe there was some perv eavesdropping outside my apartment. After all, there were a few nutty neighbors who lived in my building. But there wasn't anyone there. "So, you didn't hear that either?" I frowned.

"Move!" She pushed me out of the way. "I'm going back to Johnny Ray's before they close. Maybe I can find a real man who knows how to satisfy a real woman."

"Whoa... whoa...whoa... hey, don't forget your cat!" I shouted.

"That's your cat now, asshole!" She continued towards the elevator, fuming.

"What the hell!" I mumbled. I only rescued the cat to help myself get laid. I didn't want to keep the damn thing. When I walked back into the house there it was again. It was perched on my leather sofa staring at me; like it knew I didn't want it there. But I wasn't going to deal with this shit tonight. So, I shut my bedroom door and went to bed.

The next morning before I left to work, I didn't want to be a dick. So, I poured some water into a bowl and set it on the floor; just in case the cat got thirsty. The rescue cat was sitting on the couch sleep, or it looked like it was sleep. Cats never seem like they're actually sleeping, just pretending until they're ready to pounce. I also cracked the window so that he could get some fresh air and maybe even just run away.

"Flandy!" My elderly neighbor Mrs. Toombs was out front of the building yelling for her cat. I smiled trying to speed up so that she wouldn't talk me to death first thing in the morning.

"Jackie!"

I hated being called Jackie. "It's just Jack, Mrs. Toombs." I forced my mouth to grin.

"Jackie, have you seen my sweet little Flandy? She didn't come in for dinner last night and I'm worried."

"No, but I'll keep an eye out for her." I shrugged.

"Thank you, Jackie," she smiled.

She looked pleasingly at my butt. She was the buildings cougar. Every building has one; some lonely widow who refused to settle down. And they usually came with their dead husband's money. She was a freaky old lady, too. Jorge in the next building told me she liked to take her dentures out and perform oral sex on young guys. I'm not sure how he knew that, but I literally prayed to never become so drunk or desperate enough to find out.

Another humid day in New York City. I was oily and sticky by the time I got to work. So of course, I had to change shirts. Work was its usual monotony of people making demands and needing everything done right then. My colleagues were nice enough, I guess. They had families, children, mortgages, and student loans, so their work routines rarely deviated. They were people-bots who came with elbows. They never thought outside of the box. And if they had an opinion, it was because Mr. Hogan gave it to them.

One day I was going to start my own ad agency, hire all my co-workers that I liked, and make it a stress-free environment. There would be no cubicles. I'd have music playing, too. And there would be a big lounge area where the guys could have a couple of beers, in the middle of the day, if they wanted. And I'd hire really sexy women. But they'd have to be smart though. And I'd call them into my office and pour them a shot of whiskey. No Scotch... no bourbon and...

"Jack!"

"Sir?" Mr. Hogan interrupted my daydream and was hawking over my desk.

"What are you working on?" He glanced down at my folders.

"I was jotting down some ideas about..."

"Great! Drop this off in a mailbox on your way out. It's been sitting on my desk all day. I've got to get home and let my dog out. My wife went to yoga or some shit and..."

"Cat food," I blurted out.

"What?" Mr. Hogan frowned.

"Sorry sir. You just reminded me that I forgot to feed that cat."

"Humm... you've got a cat?" He asked.

"Sort of," I grunted.

"That's interesting," he smiled. Something he rarely did. "Never figured you for an animal lover, Jack."

"Well, animals are people too," I grinned. I was so full of shit that the fake smile I gave him stuck to my face.

"Exactly!" He nodded. "That's how I feel about my little Snookum's, Zoë. She's the sweetest little Chihuahua you've ever seen. I know you're a cat person. And I respect that. But dogs are more loving and caring you know?"

'Yes,' I nodded.

"No offense, but cats don't give a fuck about nobody but themselves. When you're ready to come over to our side, the dog lovers' side, you let me know. I'll put you in touch with the same breeder my wife got our little Snookum's from, okay?"

"Sure." Again, with the nod.

He paused. "You know, I was just thinking. How would you like to work on that new Purina Dog Food account? You, being a pet owner may be able to bring a fresh perspective; you know?"

I was speechless. But I was able to nod my head 'yes'- still wearing that stupid grin.

"Get the file from Ramsey upstairs in the morning." He walked off.

"Oh," he pivoted. "What's your cat's name?"

The smile immediately walked off my face as I scrambled for a sensible name. "Lucas!" I blurted out.

Mr. Hogan grinned. "Man, that would've been a great name for a dog." He looked at his watch and walked off.

I did my celebratory fist pump. I had closed two insignificant accounts that morning. Both with funny jingles. But they garnered a 'good job Jack' from my boss. And now, by 6:00pm he was giving me a tremendous account. The bonus on a big-time account like Purina would be at least 10 times my paycheck.

After I dropped his package in the mailbox, I stopped by my favorite watering hole to get a drink or two. It was slim pickings in there. The women looked exhausted and desperate, which is okay sometimes, but jeeesh! Tonight, they completely lacked sex appeal. Frankly, they just weren't fuckable. A couple of them looked like they should've been buying me drinks.

The owner of Johnnie Ray's was my friend Ray; a laid-back Black guy who dressed like he was ready for a G.Q. photoshoot. Ray said his grandfather told him to always dress for success; and he did, even before he became successful. He moved out of my building a year after I arrived. We used to barhop on Saturday nights until he opened his own bar, which was great because most of my drinks are free. But I really think we stopped hanging out because of his fiancée; Toni Logan. After he met her, he started making up more reasons than the law allowed- to stay home on weekends. It seemed boring if you asked me. But as long as he was happy, I was happy for him.

"I don't see any gullible college girls here tonight." Ray mockingly surveyed the room. He knew the type of women I preferred.

"I know right!" I agreed. "But it's still early."

"Congrats on your promotion, too!" He took a shot of vodka and hit his glass against mine."

"It's not a promotion. It's a big account. But not a promotion," I replied. I didn't want to be misleading.

"Speak it into existence, my friend. Besides, as long as you don't fuck this up, a promotion is coming," Ray smiled.

He was usually right. "Guess who I saw coming out of The Pretzel Factory the other day?" I laughed just thinking about it.

"Who?" he asked.

"Marty," I replied.

"Marty...Marty? Our Marty?" He frowned.

"Yep."

"We haven't seen him in months. Was he in jail? His phone was turned off and he moved from downtown." Ray shook his head.

"No," I sighed. "Apparently he's been at home eating. Dude gained about 30 pounds." I held my hand in front of my stomach to help detail how much weight our old running mate had actually picked up.

"Goddamn," Ray was stunned.

"Yeah. He's got the family-man stomach now. And the family-man van too," I said.

"What?"

"Yeah, he traded his Charger in for some new Astro-van SUV. He said his wife didn't think a Charger was right for a family-man," I explained.

"That's a damn shame! What kind of woman would make a man give up his most prized possession? She's got his nose wide-the-fuck open," said Ray.

"That's going to be you this time next year," I laughed.

"Shiiiit...! Never that!" He touched his chiseled abs. "God wants me to keep this six- pack." He stared at the front door then frowned. "And stay away from that girl in the red shirt."

"What girl in the red shirt," I repeated.

"The blond who just walked in." He pointed to a cute little thing wearing spandex.

She was 5'5" 110 lbs. of pure sexiness. Her skirt was short. Her smile was wide. Her red tank-top was low cut, and she had a slutty disposition. "Oh yeah, bout time," I smiled. **'Stiff John'** immediately woke up.

"No....no...no," said Ray. "Why do you think I'm telling you to stay away from her, dumbass? My bar back said she gave his ass the clap."

"That little hottie over there is burning?" I pointed in disbelief. "You're not just trying to cock block me, are you," I asked.

"Dude, I heard the motherfucker in the bathroom pissin' razor blades the other day, okay!"

I nodded and turned back around in my chair.

"I've got to take care of some business. I'll holla at you tomorrow." He gave me a fist bump.

"Wait, let me ask you something," I frowned with curiosity. "Can you catch Chlamydia through a condom?"

"Dude, are you serious right now?" Ray stared at me in awe.

"I'm just kidding, okay?" I laughed.

He shook his head and walked off. But I really was... kidding; mostly anyways. Although I started wondering what it would be like to wear two condoms at the same time. I glanced over my shoulder to see that my hypotheticals didn't matter. The woman in the red top was now surrounded by three hippie-looking dudes with biker tattoos.

I wanted to leave but **'Stiff John'** was forcing me to stay. So, I slow walked a beer and two shots of rum. I was killing time until something worth taking home walked through the door. But it didn't. Minutes turned into hours. I must have listened to every song on the jukebox. So, I left empty handed. I had to go home and feed that cat. I had a couple of cans of tuna in the cabinet. For a guy who wasn't going to get laid tonight, I was still pretty upbeat. I had a nice buzz, and I already had some great ideas for that Purina account.

When I walked through the door my stomach sank. There sat that black, hairy, Persian cat; the cat I had reluctantly rescued from a disgusting dumpster. The cat I was worried about not eating all day, was sitting on the floor next to my neighbor's cat, Flandy. But Flandy was dead. Her throat appeared to be ripped open as she lay in a pool of her own blood. And the cat I had just named Lucas was licking blood off his paws. It gave a whole new meaning to 'look what the cat dragged in'.

Let's Party

I stood in the doorway for almost a minute trying to figure out what the hell was going on. Meanwhile, that creepy ass cat walked over to the window and leaped out. He climbed menacingly onto the fire escape.

"Did you do this?" I yelled like an angry pet owner -although I wasn't. His fluffy tail swayed slowly- back and forth.

"What the hell do you think?"

A clear, masculine voice responded. It was the same voice from last night I heard laughing. The same pitch. The same tone. A nervous pain shot through my abdomen. Who the fuck was in my house? I stared anxiously down the hall towards my bedroom. The door was partially cracked. I couldn't remember if that was how I left it. The bathroom door was shut. Did I close it this morning?

I grabbed the biggest knife I saw from my kitchen cutlery set and went to investigate. I intentionally left the front door cracked; just in case I needed to run out fast. I didn't want to fidget with the doorknob. Cautiously, I searched my bedroom; prepared for some fiending drug addict to jump out at me. The closets and hideaways were clear. I opened the bathroom door; nothing.

"Great!" I was relieved. But I was hearing things. I chalked it up to an overactive imagination. That was my reasoning. That was how I would be able to get through the next hour... the next day... the next week without checking myself into Bellevue.

I hurried to close my front door. I shut and locked my window as well. I didn't want that giant fur-ball sneaking back in. I was hoping nobody got off the elevator and saw Mrs. Toombs' cat Flandy dead on my living room floor. That would be a huge headache I didn't need. I grabbed about five trash bags and a pair of work gloves I sometimes used whenever my trash can became extra nasty. I didn't know how pet owners disposed of their dead pets in New York, but I was going to throw Flandy into the dumpster out back. She wasn't my cat. She wasn't my problem. And that oversized fur-ball that killed her didn't belong to me either. But here I was in the middle of this weird- God knows what- shit.

When I tossed the trash bag into the dumpster, I felt kind of bad; like I should have said a few words or something. But what could I do? Who would believe I came home and found a dead cat in my apartment? That's right; nobody! If I told Mrs. Toombs what happened, the whole building would think I was some kind of weirdo or animal hating sadist. My mouth was going to remain shut. I cleaned the blood off the carpet and went back to Ray's in time for the afterhours patrons. That's when the bar was usually the most crowded. I needed another drink.

"I'm surprised nobody heard a couple of Alley cats in your living room fighting. You know the male cat, those big Tomcats, are pretty aggressive towards the females in heat," said Ray, pouring himself a drink along with mine. "I never thought you were a cat person though."

"I'm not a cat person, geez," I frowned. "This wouldn't have happened if that drunk lady hadn't bought that cat to my house."

"No, it wouldn't have happened if you weren't always thinking with your dick," Ray frowned, always in lecture mode.

"Yeah... maybe," I shrugged. "I'm a young, single, healthy, super sexy, hetero-male living in New York City. What am I supposed to be doing?" I smiled.

"Well, Mr. super-sexy, as a bartender, slash sociologist I'd tell you to sow your wild oats young man! But as your friend, I'd tell you to get a cute girlfriend and give your dick a rest, okay?"

"Someone's got Toni all in their ear," I laughed. His fiancé's words were coming out of his mouth. Women hate it when guys have single friends; afraid they'd lead them into temptation.

"Fuck you, Jack! I can think for myself," he laughed.

I put twenty dollars on the counter. Ray looked down at the money then back up at me. A smirk appeared on his face. The self-styled sociologist already knew what I wanted. Therefore, he also knew everything he said went into one ear and out the other.

"Let me guess; those two wholesome All-American girls at the end of the bar?" He nudged his head in their direction.

"I stared at him with a slow, sneaky nod. "Yep, how did you guess?" I joked. My own drinks were usually free. But whenever I was hitting on one of his patrons, I always paid for her drinks. To do otherwise would be me taking advantage of our friendship.

About a minute after Ray gave them their drinks, I wasted no time. I walked casually down to the end of the bar. Although I stepped slowly- like I could care less, inside I was hurrying; before some other guy popped up and took the nearest bar stool. My sexy, new acquaintances and I consumed more drinks. We ate countless hot wings; Ray's hot wings were the best. We played two games of darts and a few games of pool; in which I let them win. Women feel empowered whenever they're able to beat a man at something; any-thing. It made me appear more vulnerable; less threatening. Within two hours, they were ready to go back to my place.

Who Let That Cat In?

The whole dead cat thing had me feeling a little off. I was glad I had someone to keep me company. But tonight, I had two someone's. Two incredibly attractive twenty-somethings with pretty faces, tight jeans, and nice asses to fill those jeans. And as an added bonus; enough alcohol in their systems to squash all their inhibitions. Or at least I thought.

"You really believed you were going to screw both of us?" asked Chrissy smiling. The liquor had loosened her tongue. She was the taller one with the bigger breasts.

"No... No...I...I... thought we'd all just cuddle a bit and get some sleep," I answered, trying to hide my smirk.

"Judging from the lump in your pants, I doubt if sleep is what you had in mind," she pointed boldly at my crotch.

When I looked down, **Stiff John** was bulging and now I felt unusually awkward.

"Chris stop it!" The petite one named Jen laughed. "You're making him feel uncomfortable." They whispered to each other like the girls in high school used to do. "We're going to have a little night cap and cuddle. Nothing's going to happen." We headed to my bedroom. "I'll leave the door cracked in case you need something," she told her friend.

"Well, I'm going to be on the couch with this remote and this leftover whiskey," answered Chrissy. "Call me if you need help, girl," she laughed.

We laid in my bed watching YouTube videos on our phones. "I just want you to hold me, alright?" Jen whispered and snuggled up close to me.

I held her alright. I held her in at least five different positions. And for a little thing she had a lot of energy. She had me sweating like I was in a sauna. My explosion was fantastic and so was hers. We definitely cuddled after that.

The night had been outstanding! It was way better than Marge or Mandy or whatever the old truck- driving lady's name was. My face contorted just thinking about her and how desperate I was that night. Although I was hoping for a threesome, fact is, I would've had sex with either of them. But I preferred the short petite one. She was more reserved. Her friend Chrissy seemed to be the aggressive type. They tended to be more demanding in the bedroom, too.

I dozed off to sleep with this little hottie's body wrapped around mine. I was basking with satisfaction in myself and my skillfulness as a player. My bachelor pad was my playground. I was King of the merry-go-round, see-saw, monkey bars...

Stiff John had been awakened by my new little vixen's hand. Apparently, my sexy house guest wanted more. And I was delighted to oblige. She climbed on top of me, straddling and moving her toned thighs across my pelvis like a pro. She took my hands and placed them on her breasts. Then, around her throat. I squeezed gently, rubbing, and caressing her shoulders and neck. Then, like a television commercial in the middle of your favorite movie, a voice interrupted my euphoria:

"Squeeze her neck harder!"

I opened my eyes and surveyed the room. Aside from myself and Jen no one was there. My bedroom door was still ajar. The blue lights from my living room television seeped through the door. It had to be her friend Chrissy watching some chick flick.

"Squeeze harder!" The manly voice commanded.

"Did you hear that?" I whispered, still mindful of her friend in the next room.

"Yessss!" She whispered back. "You feel so good!"

Obviously, she didn't know what I was talking about. It had to be the television. And I had to ignore it. Jen's body felt so good, so right. She was riding me. Her eyes closed and head up facing the ceiling. Her silhouette pressed against mine was perfect. And her moves; erotic. I was rubbing all over her body; memorizing each curve just in case I'd never see her again. That's when my elbow touched something metal next to me in bed. I ran my hand across the cold object. It was a butcher knife. I looked down and recognized it as the biggest knife in my cutlery set.

What the fuck? I thought; still trying to maintain my erection, still trying to satisfy this woman without these weird distractions.

"Oh, baby it's here!" She whispered, referring to her orgasm.

"Oh God!" I followed, having feelings of my own.

"Stab her with that knife when you orgasm, Jack. It will be the greatest feeling you've ever had."

That voice. The knife. The prompting. That wasn't the television in the next room.

Jen's long, climatic moan of pleasure filled the air. But there was something else filling the room too, negative energy. It was everywhere.

I was satisfied physically. But mentally, I was all over the place. Who was telling me these horrible things? Was my mind playing tricks on me? I rolled over to dispose of the condom. I hated keeping them on when I was done. When I flicked on the light next to my bed, I jumped in astonishment. That large, black cat was at the foot of my bed. His red eyes staring through me. It's back arched like it was anticipating my inevitable hostility.

"How the fuck did this cat get in here?" I yelled. Just thinking about having sex with such a feral looking animal in the room made my skin crawl.

Jen jumped up in astonishment. "What's wrong? Why are you yelling?" She stretched and adjusted her eyes to the light. "Aw, that's so sweet. I didn't know you were a cat person?"

"Goddamn, I'm not! How'd that cat get in my room?" I stared at it while it stared back at me, as I kept my distance.

"How should I know?" Jen shrugged. "That's not your cat?" She asked.

"Hell no!" I replied emphatically.

Her friend Chrissy tapped at the partially open, bedroom door. "Hey guys, everything all right?" She came in and stared at me. She smiled and gave me an admiring kind of look. I forgot I was naked. I didn't really care but out of respect for Jen I took a pillow and put it in front of me.

"No, everything is not all right. How did that cat get in here?" I pointed.

"It was on your fire escape, scratching at the window. I let him in," she shrugged.

"That's not my Goddamn cat. That cat is dangerous and probably has all kinds of diseases," I yelled.

"Dude, you had a bowl sitting on the floor," she frowned. "But okay... sorry. Don't have a heart attack. I'll take him back outside so you two can get back to your fun," she smiled at her friend, then reached down to pick the unwanted guest up.

The cat's long, sharp claws immediately extended. It scratched the shit out of the unsuspecting woman. "Owww...fuck!" She yelled. "What the hell is wrong with your cat?" She looked at the deep wound that could possibly take a few stitches.

"Damn!" I gasped. I'd never seen a cat act so viciously. It then walked casually back into the living room area.

"Jen, did you see that?" Chrissy held the top of her left hand. Then showed her friend the three-inch cut with blood leaking from it.

"Jesus!" Jen's eyes bulged. "You're going to have to get that looked at." she hurried and put her clothes back on.

I grabbed two towels out of the bathroom closet. One for me and the other for her bloody hand. I told her to press down hard. The three of us peeked cautiously down the hallway to see where the cat was before we exited my bedroom.

"I'm taking you to the ER," said Jen.

"I'm sorry I opened your window," said Chrissy. Her eyes filled with water. "I'm so stupid." Clearly the alcohol was making her overly emotional.

Then Jen gave me the most beautiful smile. "I had a great time tonight." She took my wrist grinning like a giddy schoolgirl. She wrote her cell number in the palm of my hand with a sharpie. "I'd like to see you again," she whispered so that Chrissy couldn't hear. She didn't want to seem unsympathetic.

I nodded gleefully as I shut the door behind them. But I couldn't dwell on the hot, young thing that just got out of my bed. My thoughts immediately went back to the sinister voice I heard in the bedroom, with its eerie instructions. Did the girls put something in my drink? Even if I was hallucinating, the knife next to me was real enough. And I sure as hell didn't put it there. Maybe my apartment was haunted? Maybe the ghost of some asshole former tenant wanted his room back? Or maybe that dirty, black cat was the God-damn devil!

Stubborn Cats Scare Me

I pushed the window to the fire escape all the way up. "Here... Kittie...Kittie...Kittie!" I said nicely, alleviating any hostility from my voice. I knew that animals could since anger and aggression. But the cat didn't move. It sat down on its stomach and stared at me.

"God dammit, you're getting the hell out of here!" I yelled. I grabbed the broom from the kitchen and moved slowly towards it. I was extremely cautious. I didn't want to get scratched and stitched up like Chrissy.

"Come on...come on Kittie!" I said softly while trying to nudge the damn thing towards the window. But it didn't budge. It didn't hiss. It didn't even flinch. It looked at me with its red pupils shining. It sat firm like a porcelain statue. And if it were human, I imagine there would be a smirk on its face for making me look so stupid. The cat tilted its furry head to one side as if it was analyzing me; trying to figure me out. This was no ordinary cat. I could see that. Sure, it had the normal characteristics of a feline; suspicious, curious, and always licking and lounging. But something was off. Something wasn't right.

Stubborn cats scare me. If you stomp your feet, they won't spook. If you pick up a stick, they won't run. It's like they're daring you to do something. And forget about yelling; it's useless. They just keep on walking to wherever the hell they're going.

"Fuck it!" I gave up. "I'm calling animal control on your ass to-morrow." I wagged my finger at it. "Goddamn demon!" I muttered and hurried into my bedroom, locking the door in disgust.

The next morning, I woke up wishing I were more like my father. He was the superintendent for a major builder in New Jersey. He would've put on a pair of work gloves, collared that cat and tossed it out of the window. But I was scared to go near the damn thing. I didn't get much sleep either. Sometimes, I swear I heard scratching at the bottom of my bedroom door. It was unnerving. I couldn't tell if I was dreaming or if that furry demon was torturing me.

Work was mundane, as usual. And as usual the highlight of my day was seeing Lauren Tisdale. Since I was assigned to the Purina Dog Food account, she'd stop by to check my progress and leave. She was busy so I understood. She would smile at me sometimes when she was talking, in a professional way of course. I'd written down my best ideas and went to work on them; everything from dramatic skits to poster boards and catchy jingles.

Sometimes I'd find myself fantasizing about women. Women I may have met in the elevator or in the break room cafeteria. Unlike the real world, they were always sexy and compliant. Their bodies were perfect, and we were usually in my bedroom. But my favorite daydreams were of the women I had already been with. And for whatever reason we lost touch. But their scent would sometimes creep into my mind a lot. I found myself thinking about Jen; her sexy body and firm breasts gave me an erection just reminiscing about them. We texted each other a couple of times since the other night. But I could tell she was a bit standoffish because of that cat scratching the shit out of her friend.

"I see you're busy," A soft voice interrupted my thoughts.

"Huh!" I looked up, pleasantly surprised. It was Lauren Tisdale.

"Hey," she smiled. "Purina wants to change the advertising theme midstream. They want something more subtle, more family oriented."

"But we've already worked on some good material. It's what they asked for," I complained.

"I know, but it's their money, so. I jotted down some of the key details they wanted included and was hoping we could meet after work and iron them out." She stared at me with a look that prevented me from saying no.

"Sure...okay!" I stared at her perfect teeth and pouty lips.

"Good! You familiar with Johnny Ray's Bistro up the street from here?" She asked.

Wow! My favorite watering hole, I smiled. "Yeah, I go there sometimes," I nodded.

"Can you meet me there about 6:00, 6:30?" She asked.

"Sure!" I continued nodding my head like a dumbass.

"Cool. I'm late for a meeting. Talk to you later." She waved and walked away leaving me to suck up her expensive perfume.

I was in awe as I watched her trot off in her tight, red skirt and high heels- that highlighted her perfectly round ass. I was stoked just knowing I'd soon be sitting across the table from the most sought-after woman in the building. For the next few hours, I found myself staring at the Roman numerals on the clock across from me. I pulled my phone in and out of my pocket as I fixated at my desk. The cubicle seemed small now; like I'd outgrown it. I'd been working my ass off. I'd been getting things done. And I was getting noticed.

Lauren Tisdale was a class act. I wouldn't dare try any of the moves on her that I put on those drunk housewives, college girls, and barflies. Besides, she was the boss's daughter. She shared her last name with the guy whose name was on the building. And If I wanted to keep my job, I had to remain professional. I also had to make sure **Stiff John** was on his best behavior.

Me, Stiff John, and the Boss's Daughter

I arrived early to get the jump on the happy hour crowd. I wanted that cozy table in the corner of the bar. It was a dimly lit booth with comfortable chairs, just feet away from the kitchen. I told Ray once Lauren arrived to send over beer, wine, and liquor. It was my way to cover all my bases and show her I wasn't a cheapskate. Women hate cheap men. If anything kept a man from getting laid, it was being a cheapskate; penny pinching as my dad liked to call it. He taught me any man who was too stingy to show a woman a good time deserved to go home alone.

To keep from being overly aggressive, I kept reminding myself that this was a business meeting between two colleagues, not one of my clumsy attempts to get laid. When she arrived, I felt a bit nervous. There was an uncomfortable type of guilt taking place between me and my dick, **Stiff John**. I had so much lust built up inside of me for this woman, I had to really control my thoughts in order not to get an erection. She had been my fantasy since day one. The woman every man in the building wanted to sleep with. My subconscious was already searching for ways to turn this from a business meeting into one of my scores, my biggest conquest. But I ignored the signs.

"You're here early. I hope you weren't waiting long," a soft, familiar voice broke into my thoughts.

When I glanced up my eyes got stuck on her lips and the gloss that covered them. How did she look so good this late in the evening? "No, but I took the liberty of ordering those drinks. I hope you don't mind."

The server put the glasses on the table. "That was thoughtful," she smiled and set her briefcase down casually. She quickly surveyed the room. "It's kind of dark back here. Are you going to be able to see?" she asked.

"Yes, but I could get another table if you like?"

"Humm," she sighed. "It's kind of cozy, actually," she shrugged, and pulled out two file folders bulging with paperwork. "Alright, let's get to work."

We exchanged ideas for over an hour. She drunk draft beer like one of the guys; sipping her suds through a straw. It looked super sexy too. As it turned out, she was more than just a pretty face attached to a dynamite body. She was intelligent and down to earth; not snobby or dismissive. She listened to my ideas and welcomed my input. And she had a great sense of humor, too. In less than an hour we'd made great headway.

After watching us for a while Ray walked over with a curious look on his face. "Hey, can I get you guys some hot wings?"

"This is the owner. My buddy Ray," I smiled. Ray shook her hand gently. "And this is my colleague, Lauren Tisdale."

"Nice to meet you," she replied. "But no thanks. Next time," she answered, pushing her shoulder length, blonde hair to one side. She stood up and began putting her papers back into her briefcase. "I love your bar. I've been here a couple of times. And yes, the wings are delicious."

"Well, thanks," smiled Ray. "So, you guys work closely together, huh?" He looked at me with a smirk. He was clearly fucking with me. He was trying to make me laugh and embarrass myself.

"Yes, we're on different floors but we're working on this new ad campaign and Jackie here has some excellent ideas," she smiled."

"Well, I've never heard anybody call you Jackie before; other than your mom," Ray laughed.

Lauren also laughed. "Well, I like Jackie. But if you'd prefer..."

"No... No... It's fine," I blurted out. Ray smiled at me in a heckling kind of way. He knew how much I hated being called Jackie. But it sounded so sweet coming from her mouth that I couldn't help but agree.

"Well, it was nice meeting you ma'am," said Ray. "Stop by anytime." Then he just stood there bobbing his head annoyingly; again, fucking with me.

"I will," she replied. And gathered up her things.

I began to feel a certain kind of way. The business meeting had concluded. I didn't want her to leave. And neither did **Stiff John**. "I was just thinking..."

"Don't do it!" She said softly.

"I was just going to..."

"Resist the urge," she stared and extended her hand for me to shake. "It's been a very productive evening. Let's not ruin it," she sighed.

I shook her hand gently. Then watched her slowly walk away. She didn't look back like most women who wanted to know if a guy was looking at their ass. She already knew I was watching. In fact, everybody was watching. Even guys who were with their girls were watching her out the corners of their eyes. And oh, what an eye-full!

I never thought that a woman in a skirt and blazer could look so hot. When I managed to unglue my eyes from her round ass Ray was standing next to me.

"Dude, she's way out of your league," he teased.

"I know," I mumbled. "I know."

"So how did it go? " He asked.

"Good!" I grinned.

"You didn't put any of your old, cheap moves on her, did you?" he asked.

"No, I was strictly business, buddy," I answered.

"Well then..." Ray patted me on the back. "Here's a double shot of tequila. You earned it."

I was feeling good. So, I gulped down a couple more double shots of tequila after that. I hooked up with some women at the bar and the festivities continued. I was buying drinks and eating wings, eating wings, and buying drinks. I struck out when I tried to take them home. They left in an Uber and me on foot. Usually, me and **Stiff John** would be a bit salty if we didn't get laid at the end of the night. But tonight, I was feeling too good to give a shit.

My Mind's Playing Tricks on Me

I lamely stumbled off the elevator. I couldn't help but chuckle a bit because my feet were feeling heavy, but I had made it home. By the time I stuck the key in my apartment door my head was spinning like a merry-go- round. I fell on the living room carpet and continued laughing. I was surprised that my inebriated body wasn't sitting in a drunk tank at the 54th precinct, next to some guy who'd just pissed in his pants. My hand grazed my dick which immediately came to attention. Usually when I was this drunk, I had a hot woman for **Stiff John** to fall asleep inside of. I started to call Jen, but it was about two in the morning. Plus, I didn't want her to start thinking we were an item. Late night rendezvous can be tricky when it came to women getting emotionally attached.

A light breath of wind blew across my face. It wasn't a cool breeze but instead a musty, tainted puff of air from the alleyway out back. I forgot my kitchen window was still open. The curtain blew back-and-forth as un-fresh air swept through the apartment. I sighed thinking about how stupid it was to leave the window open with the a/c on. Then... *'what the fuck... what the fuck...'*

Now I remembered why I left the window open. I'd forgotten about my unwanted house guest. The furry intruder that had my nerves on edge. I lay on the living room floor ready to crawl into the bedroom when I caught a glimpse of a dark, four-legged shadow-creeping around my dimly lit kitchen. It was walking towards me. I was too damn drunk to stand up and run, then again what would I be running from? It's just a big, grubby- old alley cat, right?

Then I remembered that nasty scratch it gave Jen's friend Chrissy. Her hand could be infected right now. "Fuck!" I got up hastily, stumbling down the hallway watching the room spin. I fell just short of my bedroom door and puked next to the doorway. Goddamn, I hadn't thrown up after a night of drinking in over three years.

"You're pretty wasted, huh?" A voice as clear as the vodka I'd polished off earlier, was speaking to me.

"Here we go again?" I mumbled.

"I wish I could drink. It looks fun. But felines get ethanol poisoning. I'd end up shitting all over your nice carpet and you'd hate me even more than you do now," the voice continued.

I sat up as sober as a judge; propped up by my elbow, I smiled. It was that same weird voice from the other night. I was hearing things again but at least this time I was good and drunk. That wicked looking cat was about 3 ft' from my face. It was licking its paws. And staring at me like it wanted something. Or wanted me to do something.

"I figure now is as good a time as any to reveal myself," the hidden voice continued.

It was inside my head. I even covered my ears, but it wouldn't go away. I remember locking my front door after I came in. My keys were in my pocket. I didn't leave the television on. And the battery in my cell phone had died, so I hadn't pocket-dialed anyone. It was only me in my apartment, laying down watching that nuisance cat...right?

"Somebody must have put something in my drink," I laughed. I don't believe in ghosts. "And cats don't talk." I stared into its red eyes. "And they certainly wouldn't talk to me if they did," I mumbled.

"I wouldn't categorize what I'm doing as talking, Jack. I'm communicating. It's like a higher frequency of what humans commonly called telepathy," was the reply.

"Telepathy," I laughed. "Yeah, sure!" I glanced over at the pile of puke I left in the corner. "Umph...umph...umph," I'll get that up tomorrow. I rubbed my bubbling stomach. And begin to crawl towards my bed.

"Wait!" The voice said. At the same time, the cat took a few more steps towards me. *Coincidence?*

"You're right. That shit stinks! Chicken and barbecue sauce. You were supposed to eat before you drink. Coat your stomach. Not the opposite way around," it said. The cat was staring right at me. Its mouth wasn't moving but I felt something odd about it. Cats always creeped me out. "Get the hell away from me!" I kicked my legs at it.

"If you kick me, I'll scratch the shit out of you like I did that bitch you had over here the other night," the voice said sternly.

I was dumbfounded and fearful at the same time. "Cats don't talk!" I blurted out. "God get that voice out my head and I'll never drink again, I swear." My head started spinning faster. My stomach was queasy, and I was ready to throw up again. All I wanted to do was lock my door and go to sleep. "Well, if you can read my mind then what am I thinking right now?" I asked.

"Probably, fuck me!" it answered.

And it was right too. "Black cat...demon...be gone! The blood of Christ compels you!" I gulped. "Help me Mary... Jesus... Pope John Paul," I blurted out.

"I'm only kidding. I can't read your mind, Jack. It was a lucky guess because that's what I would've been thinking." It casually licked its paws.

I reached for the light switch. "Leave it off. The light hurts my eyes," it ordered. I rubbed my stomach, hoping it would help me avoid throwing up again. "What do you want from me?" I asked.

"I need somewhere to stay and lie-low for a few days. I don't want them to find me," it paced back and forth; only stopping twice to look at me with its red, haunting eyes. It displayed all the normal functions of a cat; the sudden moves, the twitching, the licking, stopping, and staring; the overall scary eeriness.

"Who's looking for you; animal control...PETA...SPCA?" I asked.

"Them. The aliens who did this to me," the voice answered.

"You've got Mexicans after you," I laughed. "Okay, well... I'll call immigration in the morning if you let me get some sleep," I said sarcastically.

The cat hissed angrily. It stared at me- frozen in my doorway like a hairy stature. "Don't be an asshole, Jack. You know what kind of aliens I'm talking about," the voice said sternly.

"Aliens," I grunted. Oh my God am I really this drunk?" I mumbled.

"You're drunk, but this is happening, Jack. Deal with it," It replied.

"Wait, you killed my neighbor's cat, Flossy," I frowned.

"I've killed way more cats than that; among other things," it replied. "It's a defect, Jack. It's a side effect of whatever it is they did to me. Along with this telepathy comes a need to kill other cats... dogs... animals. I even get euphoric watching humans hurt and kill each other. And I know it's not normal." it said.

I kept watching this menacing cat- walk in and out of the shadows around my room; occasionally smelling socks, shoes and other items that were scattered about the floor. It sat. It stood. It licked. It paced. Its expressionless face stared directly at me while a voice, possibly its voice, remained resident in my head. There were no wires or speakers. There was nothing that would suggest this was a clever prank. Wherever that voice was coming from it was stern and intimidating. My already throbbing headache was magnified by its serious tone. I covered my ears hoping it would stop. But it was like having my earbuds in and the volume on my phone turned up high.

"They're looking for me Jack. They want to continue their experiments." The persistent feline continued to pace...continued to stare into my drunk, tired, watery eyes.

My hallucination just got more ridiculous. But then again, why not aliens? I already had a talking cat trying to live rent free in my head. I wanted it to stop. I needed sleep. "Oh God, why me?" I sighed.

"You helped me so I'm going to help you. Consider me a whistleblower."

"Okay. But I need some air. I'm still feeling dizzy, you know. Let's go out on the fire escape." I stood up and headed slowly down the hallway. And the cat, like most cats ran ahead of me. But as soon as it got out of my bedroom I shut and locked my door. It scratched at the door angrily.

"You dumbass! You're really starting to piss me off, Jack!"

I made it to my bed and fell face first upon my plush mattress. I laid on my side because my headache and hangover wouldn't allow me to lay on my stomach or back. I was afraid I was going to puke all over my comforter.

I only had about four hours of sleep before my phone alarm vibrated in my pocket. My eyelids felt heavy, and my head was pounding from the hangover. My body always required at least six hours of sleep for me to function properly. But I couldn't afford to be late. I had too many eyes on me and wasn't about to fuck it up.

"Umph!" My head was pounding, and I'd slept in my clothes. It wasn't my first long night, but it had been a while. I sniffed my armpits. They smelled like cigarettes and booze. And I didn't even smoke. What the hell did I do last night? I took a hot shower with thick, cinnamon body-wash. It smelled wonderful. The steam got my blood circulating and brought me back to life. But this time it also brought something else back, last night's highlight reel. Initially, I was having problems remembering. But I got the feeling something important had happened. I rubbed an ample amount of mousse into my hair. Then grabbed two shirts and my favorite tie. I stared at my bed. Did I have company last night? Did I get laid? Naw, I've never been so drunk that I forgot getting laid. But I did need to walk back everything that happened when I got off work.

First, the meeting I had with Lauren Tisdale was a success. Her dress was an instant boner for me.

Second, after the meeting I got totally shit- faced.

Third, I partied with two out-of-towners and neither of the women gave me their phone numbers. I stumbled my way home, thank God.

Fourth, I went to bed. But...

I unlocked and opened my bedroom door. But why was it locked? Yeah, I remember vomiting on the carpet. And it stunk to high hell.

I looked down at the baseboard. "Damn," it still stunk like hell. But there was something else. Something important that I'd forgotten. I stared across the living room at my open dining room window and thought about how stupid I was to leave it open with the air conditioner running. But when I went to close it, I saw something moving out of the corner of my eye. Hoping it was just the after-effects of my wild partying night, I turned in shock. There was that cat I couldn't get rid of, perched on my kitchen countertop like he'd lived here forever. Its red eyes set like freshly polished rubies staring at me. Its wide tail danced back and forth like a fluffy pendulum. The hairy animal didn't move... didn't blink. But neither did I. It was gauging my reaction or over reaction in my case. I tripped over my peace lily plant trying to get the hell out of there. Then it came to me, my memory. That damn thing was talking to me last night... impossible? Was I dreaming? Was I hallucinating? Why did I get that drunk?

"I didn't mean to startle you. But we must talk." A voice said.

All the details were coming back to me. I was drunk last night but I'm not a fool. I remember someone was talking to me...harassing me. I looked around the living room. That cat! That big ass, dirty Persian cat was communicating with me last night. But I'm not drunk this morning. And here we are again.

"Wait!" The masculine voice in my head shouted before the cat leaped from the counter and onto the floor. I turned to flee my apartment and ran straight into the door. I was clumsy and scared. "F-u-c-k!" I rubbed my forehead.

"That's going to leave a mark." The comment was sarcastic but true.

"Cats can't talk... cats can't talk!" I mumbled, quickly getting back up.

"Oh Jesus Christ! Not that again?" The voice sounded irritated.

I ran into the hallway holding the doorknob behind me as if it could somehow open it with its paws- and follow me out. What the hell is wrong with me? This can't be real life! I peeped back inside my apartment as if I was a stranger. The cat was just sitting there, staring back at me with those fire red eyes that I'd never seen on any animal before.

"Think of me as a whistleblower, Jack. I'm trying to do the right thing here. There are some things you should know just in case they find me," it continued.

I didn't say anything. I looked up and down the narrow hallway making sure no one was watching. Then I stuck my head back in and watched cautiously.

"When you hear those stories about people getting abducted by aliens and getting probes stuck up their asses, it's usually true; give or take a nut job or two. What you don't know is that they experiment on animals too. Animals like me, Jack. They have a hidden space-craft just outside of Connecticut. A place called Dark Entry Forest, in Dudley Town. It's a dead zone that's said to be hunted. People don't camp there, or hike, or hunt there. And the ones who do go in, never come back out. But it's not haunted, Jack. It's them."

I was skeptical. Not of the cat but of my own sanity. "I got it. Aliens in Connecticut. Experiments in the dead zone. Look, I would love to stay and chat with you about this, but I have to get to work. So, I will leave the window open," as if I were going to go back in and close it, "and you could just leave. Okay. Thanks for the info. I'll alert the proper authorities and I'll stay out of Connecticut."

"This isn't a game, Jack! The entire East Coast...America...the world is in trouble. We are all just sport and entertainment for them."

"I understand. I do. But I'm late for work. So... alright then!" I closed the door and hurried to the elevator. My heart was racing.

Why was this happening to me? I had no known history of mental illness in my family. And if by some remote chance it was real, then why was it happening to me? Why did it choose me? This cat, this feline invader had traumatized me. In just a few days it had me questioning my own sanity. The cat was real enough. It scratched the shit out of Jen's friend. But was it communicating with me or a figment of my imagination? Is my mind in crisis?

As soon as I got to work, I downed four Tylenols and two cups of coffee before calling animal control. Those fuckers weren't helpful at all. They said the cat was my problem and they didn't make house calls to pick up house pets. Then the fuckers suggested that me and my cat get vaccinated. What the hell? I was beyond frustrated. I needed someone to talk to. I called my buddy Ray and told him what was going on. Of course, he was going to say I was on drugs.

"Man, you got to be high as hell to think of a story like that. I can't believe you didn't tell me this sooner. But check this out; they gave me the same shit when I was In Afghanistan. There was this fine honey I was talking to in a village outside of Kandahar. She said she could get me some real good weed right... straight fire; just like the high-grade shit we smoke here. I was like cool, baby. I gave her twenty...twenty-five bucks. About half an hour after I smoked that shit, I was feeling good...really good. Then, shit got weird. I just started walking and walking. I walked off and left my platoon. Long story short, I was in the desert for three- days watching a Michael Jackson and Prince concert that never happened."

"What?" I asked. Ray rarely if ever talked about his time fighting in Operation Desert Storm.

"Yeah, they were on stage together singing each other's songs and dancing. And you couldn't tell me that shit wasn't real, either. By the time my unit found me I was half dead, dehydrated, naked and sitting in the middle of a fucking sand dune, man. The doctor said my hallucination was a result of LSD and my subconscious mind loving music and wanting to go home. Whatever that meant." he sighed.

"So, you think I was drugged?" I asked.

"We got pretty crowded last night and there were a bunch of new faces. Have you been sweating a lot? Nauseous? Vomiting?" he questioned.

"Yeah, all that." I agreed.

"Yeah bro, sounds like LSD to me," he said.

"Fuck!" I gulped.

"Look, step one. You have got to drink plenty of water to flush your system. Then go home, lay down and sweat it out. It's kind of like weed. You just got to let it wear off," he instructed. "Did you drive to work or walk?"

"I was running late so I drove," I answered.

"Can you call an Uber and make it home?" he asked?

"Yeah," I answered looking around the room. No one was paying any attention to me. All the worker bees were busy. "Second, you got to get rid of that damn cat. That thing has way too much negative energy, dude. Now check your phone," he said.

I saw a text message alert. "Whose number is this," I asked?

"I sent you the number of this guy named Ryan. I pay him 50 bucks every couple of days to clean cans, bottles, and trash from the front and the back parking lot. He's consistent and does a decent job. I figure if you give him thirty or forty- bucks he'll snatch that cat up and take him down the street somewhere. Problem solved."

"Yeah?" I sighed a breath of relief. He had introduced an idea that was rational and plausible.

"Oh yeah," he hesitated. "Don't leave him alone in your apartment. Because I don't want you to blame me if something goes missing. He looks like one of those meth heads. His teeth are all fucked up and shit, okay."

"Okay," I laughed. I needed that laugh, too."

When Animals Attack

When I stepped off the elevator there was a tall, lanky guy with a dirty goatee waiting in front of my apartment door. His hair was matted but not from trying to grow dreads but more like from-not giving a shit about combing it. He was wearing a New York Giants t-shirt, and some withered-up shorts that were simply too big for his body. Well, at least we both like the Giants.

"I'm Ryan. You text me about a cat you need removed from your apartment?" He extended his hand.

I looked down at his fingers and nails; they were filthy. But I didn't want to seem like an asshole, so I shook his hand. The whole Covid-19, Monkey Pox thing made me wish this guy were wearing a mask.

"I'm Jack. Thanks for coming on short notice," I pushed out a dull smile.

"Cool!" he nodded.

I put the key in the door then looked at him. "Listen, about this cat...."

"Dude, I'll be gentle; okay!" He stared impatiently at me.

"It's not that..."

"You're not about to change your mind, are you? I drove all the way from..."

"No!" I blurted out. "That cat is kind of vicious and I don't want any problems," I answered.

"Look, I'm in a hurry. Can you just give me my money up front, like right now? After I snag your little feline friend, I've got some business to take care of," he said.

This guy Ryan seemed a little fidgety. "I hope you got gloves. I saw it scratch the blood out of somebody a few days ago and..."

"Dude, it's a cat. What the hell are you so afraid of?" His demeanor seemed a bit agitated. "I got gloves. But I get it. You don't like to get your hands dirty, huh? So, you call people like me?"

I handed him forty- bucks. "No!" I frowned. "This cat seems kind of vicious and..."

"Hey, don't sweat it. I'm teasing you, man." He shoved the money into his pocket and came back out with some cheap looking mitts. He held up both hands sarcastically showing his Dollar Tree gloves. "See! Next time call me when you've got a two-legged cat you need help with." He laughed and nudged my shoulder.

I shrugged and unlocked my door, thinking; *this guy is a fucking idiot*. But I wasn't going to be discourteous since the man was doing me a favor. When we walked inside, I felt uneasy. But I was glad to be finally getting rid of this pain-in-the-ass cat.

"Hey, you got a knapsack or a bag," I asked.

"No, just grab me one of your pillowcases," he looked around my apartment. He was sizing me up. "I'm guessing you can afford to buy another one," he smirked. "You're going to give me a nice tip, aren't you; for helping you out like this?" He smiled mischievously.

And there were those shiny, rotten, fucked-up teeth Ray warned me about. They looked like they were about to fall out of his head. Yeah, he was on drugs alright. He kept rubbing his neck like he had a nervous tick.

"Sure, I'll give you a few extra bucks." I hurried into the bedroom to get a pillowcase, keeping my eye on this unsavory character the entire time.

"So how long you lived here," he asked. Walking around the apartment. I knew he was making small talk, but I also knew he was scoping out the place.

"A few years," I answered, hurrying back. I had some valuable stuff, and I didn't want his filthy hands touching any of it. That's when that menacing cat walked from the kitchen and crawled under the couch.

"There's your little furball now," said Ryan. "Dam, he's really big, huh. What the hell you been feeding him?" He knelt and peered beneath the sofa. "Here Kitty...Kitty... Kitty!" He started feeling around underneath the middle section.

Then, out of nowhere, as clear as day- an angry voice said:

"Oh, you brought a fucking drug addict to handle me, huh Jack. I told you I wasn't going anywhere. I can smell the crystal meth all over this bastard."

I begin hitting my forehead with the palm of my hand. My insanity was talking to me again. I didn't want to hear anymore... that voice. I started humming like a special needs child who needed to calm down. Ryan stood back up and looked at me.

"Dude...seriously? Are you on something?" He asked. "Do you mind not doing that?"

The drug addict was asking me if I was high. What irony. I shut up, stopped fidgeting, and crossed my arms. I watched him kneel back down and wave his arm underneath the sofa.

"Where are you... you little shit?" He coughed a bit.

A few seconds later, the feral creature ran from under the sofa with its red eyes practically bulging out of the sockets. It leaped effortlessly onto Ryan's dirty face. Ryan jerked backwards in astonishment as the agile animal dug its black claws into his cheeks and scalp.

"I told you I wasn't fucking around here, Jack. Now, you're going to get your buddy here- all fucked up!" The voice yelled angrily while the cat looked at me.

Ryan sprung to his feet practically screaming. "What the fuck! Get it off!" His muffled voice sounded terrified as the cat stretched its belly across his nose and mouth. I could see it digging its sharp claws into his flesh. The more Ryan tried to pull it off the harder it clung to his face.

The frightening Persian cat looked absolutely sinister. Its wide belly covered Ryan's face like it was fastened with Velcro, making it impossible for him to breathe. I could hear it talking... taunting.

"Look what you made me do, Jack!"

"Look what you made me do, Jack!"

Its face, whiskers, and eyes look deformed; even monstrous. The hair all over its furry body pointed upwards like a husky porcupine. I was frozen with fear. I'd never seen a cat behave in such an aggressive manner; so vicious... so hateful... so deliberate. Then it opened its mouth and stuck its pointed teeth into the poor guy's forehead.

"Awwww, God damn-it!" His muffled voice was full of panic. His cheap gloves rolled off his fingers as he tugged at the cat's neck and tail. Ryan screamed, punching and pulling at the unhinged animal. But it didn't budge. It was like a furry magnet stuck to his face. He was suffocating. "I can't breathe...I can't breathe. Get it off me," he yelled with muted tone.

I ran into the kitchen and grabbed a cooking pan. But as soon as I swung to hit it, the agile animal leaped from Ryan's face, causing me to smash him square in the nose with the 8" saucepan.

"Ahhh!" Ryan yelled again.

I heard the bone in his nose crack as it connected with my favorite cookware. It sounded like someone balling up a sheet of notebook paper. Blood squirted out and rolled into his mouth. Ryan fell backwards hitting the base of his head against the knee wall that separated the kitchen from the living room. He coughed and gagged, trying to catch his breath. He slumped over on the carpet, wheezing like a child having an asthma attack.

"Goddamn!" I bulked. God knows I didn't mean to hit him. I instantly felt like shit.

"Now get the fuck out of here, Kevin... Bryan... or whatever the fuck your name is." The mean-spirited voice in my head sounded highly irritated.

"Why are you telling me to get out?" Asked Ryan. He was crying like a schoolgirl as he covered his bloody nose with his shirt. "I came here to help you," he sobbed.

"Wait...what? You heard that?" My mouth dropped open like a broken mailbox. He heard it too! I laughed. I laughed because I wasn't going nuts. Except in all the confusion he thought it was me; but it wasn't. I hurried to help Ryan up. God knows I felt awful. He pulled away.

"Get your Goddam hands off me, man! You think this is funny?" His wobbly legs stumbled to the front door. "You set me up. You knew your cat was fucking vicious," he cried as blood and mucus streamed out of his nose. Ryan wagged his finger at me angrily. "Your cat tried to kill me, man!"

"That's not my cat! "I blurted out.

"I ought to sue you!" He looked down at his whelped-up arms and chest. "Fuck you!"

As he hustled past me, I could see the tear in his jawline. The white meat was showing on one side of his face and there was a 1/4-inch-deep laceration on the other. Not to mention the teeth marks on his forehead. He was going to need a bunch of stitches, a tetanus shot, bandages, gauzes, and painkillers; although I figured he probably had the painkillers covered. He slammed the door. And I could hear him cursing all the way to the elevator.

I looked across the room at the cat. It was casually licking the blood from its legs and paws. It was back normal again; claws retracted and hair flat. I watched it from a safe distance, but I was prepared to run into my bedroom and lock the door if necessary.

This was happening whether I wanted it to or not. Whether anyone believed me or not. This cat was talking loud and clear. I wasn't crazy. I wasn't crazy at all. I wasn't drunk either. Telepathy was real. And that voice that had been invading my thoughts for days now, wasn't my imagination. Nor was it signs of mental illness. Someone else had heard it. Now, I had so many questions; who, what, why, when, and where? But what I was really thinking was; what in the hell am I going to do now?

Oh, What A Relief It Is!

At the last minute I decided to leave my apartment. I didn't want to be anywhere near that vicious animal. I didn't want to hear that voice in my head and feel my heartbeat like crazy whenever it was around. I didn't want to see Ryan's blood drops on the carpet, either. I needed time to think and compose myself. I thought it was best not to stay at my place with all the weird shit going on. I was in shock. I was confused. I was afraid; all at the same time. Stuff like this didn't happen to people like me. I'm the guy you party with.

Not the guy who solves mysteries or sticks his nose where it doesn't belong. I needed to catch my breath. I needed comfort. I had to find something hot to put my arms around and funnel all my frustration into. I wanted to grind and squeeze and hump. I was in desperate need of release. Sex always made me feel better about everything.

I pulled out my phone and scrolled through my list of one-night stands. And one name stood out, causing me to instantly reminisce: Jen. The night we spent together was fantastic. So, I called her up. She seemed happy to hear from me too. I caught the subway to her place because I knew I was going to get too fucked up to drive back home. Needless to say, **Stiff John** was excited and kept my pants bulging the entire way over there. Just thinking about squeezing Jen's ass and sucking her luscious breasts made my loins tingle with anticipation. Jen had the perfect body to make me feel better and blank out everything that happened in the last 48 hours, at least for a while anyway.

"Hi Jack." Jen squeezed me tightly. Before I could even get through the front door, she pressed her bombshell body firmly against mine. I was certain she felt that bulge in my pants, just like I'd wanted her too.

"Hi Jack... bye Jack," Jen's friend and roommate Chrissy walked past me in a hurry. She seemed a bit salty.

"Don't mind her," said Jen. "She's still pissed about the other night. She ended up getting six stitches you know."

"Damn!" I frowned and looked down at her bandaged hand. It was a bit swollen. She kept it next to her waist. Then I looked up at her breasts. They were still huge. And now that I was sober, she wasn't a bad looking woman either. But judging from the grimace look on her face, it would be impossible to talk them into a three-some now. That four-legged beast made sure of that.

"Can we just go to your room?" I took Jen's hand. "Sure, come on." She led me down the hallway and into the master bedroom. I could tell because it was bigger, more spacious than mine.

"Take your shoes off and relax," she said softly. "You're not going anywhere anytime soon." I was thinking the exact same thing.

"At first, I thought you weren't going to call me. Because everything happened so fast the other night," she explained.

We sat on the edge of her bed. **Stiff John** wanted me to just grab her, pull her pants down and go to work. I felt like a bonafide sex fiend, but I controlled myself.

"No, I've just been really busy." The small talk was bothering me.

"Well, I'm glad you called," she squeezed my face. "You don't look so good. Have you been getting enough sleep," she asked.

"Not really. I've been a little stressed about work stuff, you know?" I sighed.

"Well, let me help you relax," her soft voice whispered.

Jen must have known why I was there. She locked her bedroom door and turned on her Bluetooth. As old 80's classic rock blasted from a 6" speaker next to the bed, I mounted her from behind like a crazed mountain man. This time I didn't even care if her roommate heard us. I had to get this yearning out the pit of my stomach; this fear... this frustration... this anger. Jen's skin felt extra smooth, extra soft. Her insides were super wet. God knows it's what I needed. I smacked, pulled, and squeezed with unnecessary roughness. I took all my fear and anxiety out on her. She seemed to like it. In fact, I'd say she liked it a lot. We climaxed at the same time- both of us moaning and out of breath.

"Wow...dam!" She panted. "Can you come and see me more often when you're mad?"

We both laughed as that relaxed, after sex calmness made us cuddle. "Jen, do you believe in God?" I blurted out.

"Didn't you hear me calling him a few minutes ago?" She smiled. "That's a funny question for pillow talk, Jack. But in fact, I do."

"Really?"

"Yes. There's somebody up there looking out for us; sometimes anyway. Why? What do you think?" She asked.

"I used to think that. But can you believe in evil, supernatural occurrences happening to people and God knows about it but doesn't try to stop it?"

"Evil itself can have a natural order. And God just lets it play out. Everybody's got to believe in something, Jack. I don't believe we're all just wandering around aimlessly, spinning our wheels doing nothing, fighting...surviving...overcoming. It has to have a purpose," Jen sighed. "If not, we're just a bunch of primates and fuckups with no redeeming qualities. The belief in God helps us to evolve. Real or imagined, he's one hell of an inspirational character."

"Wow, okay, that was deep" I sighed. "I need to talk to you more often, professor," I joked.

"I'm not what you expected sober, huh? Well, if you called me more often, you'd know I take courses in philosophy and metaphysics at NYU?"

"Dam!" I smiled. "That's excellent!" I was taken aback by her intelligence. Most of the women I slept with were dummies compared to her.

"What about UFOs...aliens... telepathy? Do you believe in any of that? I asked.

"Well, yes to some degree," replied Jen.

"But how can you believe in God and aliens at the same time?"

"Easy, maybe God created them both," she shrugged.

"I don't know. Seems kind of farfetched to have both. I mean, alien knowledge would uplift society, right? Make the world unite without worrying about hell's fire, right?" I reasoned.

"I hadn't thought about that, Jack. Maybe you should come to my class sometime," she giggled. Still showing the feminine vulnerability that I liked. "Here's the thing, because of our pettiness, our selfishness, our greed; we've stifled our own growth. We've failed to evolve. If aliens were to ever come here, we'd automatically be at least a thousand years or more behind them in technology and science. It would be really arrogant of us Jack, to think that in this great, big, huge universe with planets, galaxies, milky ways, and black holes, that we were the only life anywhere. Even if there was no God it would be almost impossible for other solar systems to not have their own big bangs, creations, and evolutions." Jen had masterfully explained so much of her unique viewpoint. And it made all the sense in the world to me.

"One last question for you, Jen," I sighed.

"Okay," she sat up in bed. "You're not going to ask me how many guys I've been with are you?"

"No!" I laughed. She kept a straight face so I couldn't tell if she was joking or not. "Actually, I just wanted to know if you think those people who claim they were abducted by aliens, are crazy?"

"Some of them, yes," she answered. But others... no. I don't think they're crazy. I think there's something really happening out there. Like, we don't know why or where they were taken. But until our technology advances, we can't do much to stop these abductions from happening."

After rolling off of Jen that night I felt better and was able to get some sleep. Everything she said made sense. But I wasn't about to tell her what I'd been going through. I didn't want her to think I was a nutjob. I had to sort this thing out on my own. I spent the night and half the day with Jen. We both called in sick from work. I had to admit, it was kind of fun, too. She even made me breakfast in bed. Her roommate went to work so we had the house to ourselves. We were like teenagers whose parents were out of town. We had loud, noisy sex that morning and again that afternoon. And the more I hung around Jen the more attached I saw her becoming. Although she was full of intelligence and logic, she was like most women I knew; emotional and ready to be claimed. I understood that. She was a single woman who wanted someone steady in her life. However, I was a single man, who wanted to remain single. It was time to go.

We're Not Alone

All our lives we've heard stories about strange, unexplainable things happening to people, random disappearances, and unusual sightings. But I never once thought it could happen to me. But here I was, caught in the middle of this unexplained phenomenon. And who would've guessed a former one-night stand would give me the clarity I needed to walk back into my apartment and face this unusual fear.

It was almost 6 o'clock p.m. when I got back home from Jen's place. I felt relieved and a lot less crazy. But before I could even get into my apartment, I noticed that the front door was cracked open. I couldn't remember if I had locked it or even shut it for that matter. After the cat from hell attacked Ryan, I high tailed it out of there. I pushed the door open enough to peek inside. I was relieved to see my buddy Ray and his girlfriend Toni sitting on the couch. But how did they get in and where the fuck was that cat?

"Yo, my man! Where you been?" Ray grabbed my shoulder and shook my hand. "We were kind of concerned about you."

"Stop lying, you were worried," Toni laughed. "Talking about, *'it ain't like Jack to leave his door open. Why he ain't answering his phone?* she mimicked his voice.

"Woman, I do not sound like that," Ray laughed. "Anyway, me and bae was doing our little date night thing, and I just thought we'd stop by and check on you."

"I'm good...you know," I carefully surveyed the room.

"Why your eyes so red and puffy, man? You been crying?" He asked sarcastically.

"Funny," I sighed. "Just my allergies acting up. How long y'all been here?" I walked into the kitchen and looked out at the fire escape. The window was still open as a light breeze blew the curtain back and forth, which meant that cat was still in here, watching...listening.

"Bout twenty-minutes I guess." He walked over to me then looked back at his girlfriend to see if she was listening. "What the hell happened to Ryan? Dude looked fucked up, man."

I took a deep breath. I could feel we were being watched. I had to choose my words carefully. "It was an accident," I answered.

"An accident? What, a car accident? Come on Jack. He said you beat him with a frying pan, man. Have you seen him?"

I shook my head 'no.'

"He tried to steal some of your shit, didn't he? You can tell me. Dude came by the bar after he left the emergency room, right. His nose was all swollen and bandaged up. He had a bunch of stitches, too. The motherfucker's face was all purple and blue- and shit. He was like; 'your boy knocked out my front tooth,' man.' I was like, dam! Them shits was already brown. I didn't say that to him but I sure as hell wanted to," he laughed.

"Seriously, dude. I didn't mean to hit him like that. It was..." at that moment I looked over at Toni sitting quietly on the couch. She wasn't paying us any attention. But underneath the sofa, right next to her leg, I saw two red eyes staring out at me.

"Man, that guy's talking about filing a lawsuit," continued Ray.

Then I heard, *"get rid of them Jack. We don't have time for this."*

An immediate fluttering went through my stomach as my palms started to sweat. "You know I got that presentation to do in the morning, so I got to practice, you know?" I had to get rid of them fast.

"Oh yeah that's right, you're a big shot now," smiled Ray. "Hey baby, you know Jack just got a big promotion at work. He's gone be running shit soon, huh?"

Toni looked up and smiled. "Congratulations. You just moved another step closer to starting your own Ad agency."

"I guess," I nodded.

"You do intend to start your own business one day, don't you?" She asked.

"Um...um...um...yeah, of course," I stuttered. "I just don't want to rush it?"

The menacing black cat was lurking and watching as it crawled from one side of the couch to the other. It was impatient and agitated. Every time it blinked it reminded me of Christmas lights going on and off. Meanwhile, Toni was scrolling through her social media, unaware of the danger sitting beneath her.

"Last warning Jack. In approximately one minute I'm going to bite into this pretty woman's Achilles hill. She's going to try and run but she'll fall. Then I'm going to jump on her face and claw her left fucking eyeball out."

The voice was angry, specific, and hateful. "God damn!" I bulked. "Please...." I begged.

"Please what?" Asked Ray. They were both oblivious to the danger they were in. "What?" Ray looked at me. Then looked around the apartment for the cat. He leaned in close. "You still hearing those voices?"

I lowered my head. I didn't want to answer.

"I told you to ignore that shit, man," Ray sighed.

"Will you both please just go!" I blurted out. I was in fear. I didn't want anything to happen to either one of them.

Toni stood up and put her hands on her hips. She gave me the evil eye. "What's up with your boy? You know I didn't want to stop by here no dam way."

Ray took his girlfriend's hand and they walked quickly towards the door. He looked back at me and frowned. "Asshole!"

"I'm sorry. This pressure is seriously getting to me," I explained.

My heart was pounding knowing that at any second that sizable, Persian cat could attack my friends. As soon as the door shut behind Ray, the silhouette of the cat appeared on the wall behind the couch. Its previously arched back was back to normal, and its slow-moving gestures showed me it had calmed down.

"Jack, you remind me so much of my first owner, Paul. When you pulled me from the dumpster that night, for a second, I thought you were him. He disappeared three days before those fucking aliens got me. I believe they took him first. And he ended up in one of their fucked-up experiments. We call them 'The Grays.' And I don't know how long they've been on this planet, but they're the worst. The Grays test and experiment on anyone and anything. When the silverware is missing from your kitchen drawer, that's them. They take the silver objects like forks and spoons to practice bending them with their minds. They exercise their minds like you humans exercise your bodies.

When you drive to work and don't remember how you got there, that's them fucking with you. When you have a really bad dream that you can't seem to remember; it may not have been a dream. When you see something move out the corner of your eye but nothing's there, that's them watching you. They're not here to take over. They seem content to watch our fears and gullibility. They implant Ideas and instructions that lead us to harm, kill and murder each other, while they observe. We are their amusement, their ignorant toys. And they like watching us as much as humans like watching television. We're morbid variety shows. We're their entertainment, Jack. The world is a fucked-up, horror-filled, reality program that the government can't or won't do a dam thing about.

The voice sounded angry again.

I became a pet to one of The Grays. For some unknown reason it liked me. It held me. It coddled me like I was its pet. It fed me and took me everywhere it went. I've traveled places no being on Earth has ever been. I've seen sites that your human imagination couldn't conceive of Jack. I've stood on a planet with four moons that stretched across the horizon like a Renaissance painting. I've seen fireflies as big as dragons swarm in formations and circles that lit up the night sky. I've visited cities that defy gravity, suspended above mountains made of ice and sand. I even slept on a planet with millions of human-like beings as tiny as hand carved figurines that could fit into a child's dollhouse. Oh, I've seen life, Jack.

We cats have a heightened sense of awareness, like feline empaths. But around my alien master, I felt nothing. No matter how often it carried me in its arms like a child clinging to a teddy bear, I sensed no emotion. It held no admiration. Showed no hate. Exhibited no love. And now, in hindsight I think, it was using me to try and feel something; to capture what we animals and you humans feel towards each other. It was using me to spark or draw something that was missing from within itself. Then one day it placed me on a triangular table, waved its hand across some machine and when I woke up, I was in a dirty, pissy alley about 2 miles from here, thrown away like trash. A couple of weeks later I met you.

Now, it sounded hurt. And my head was spinning. I needed a break; a few minutes to digest everything this cat just revealed. I stood cautiously across the room, still afraid to get too close. "I need ...to...to get some air," I mumbled.

"I know Jack. This was a lot to unpack. I won't be able to answer all your questions, but I'll do the best I can when you get back."

I nodded and headed down the hall.

"Thanks for listening!" **the muffled voice said as I neared the** elevator.

Where Did He Go?

I not only needed a break, I also wanted to apologize to Ray and his girlfriend. She already didn't like me much, so I wanted to smooth things over a bit. But I didn't see Ray's car out front of my building. So, I took a few deep breaths then walked back inside. When I stepped into my apartment the energy had changed. There was an atmosphere of anxiety and fear. But it wasn't mine. I was still a bit nervous but the butterflies in my stomach were thirsty for knowledge. The wheels in my head were turning. Questions will be raised. I wanted to know more. I needed to understand the nature of his alien handlers, more about the places he'd seen. I had countless questions.

I looked across the room and saw the window to the fire escape open. The curtains blew back and forth like a horror movie waiting to happen. I was only gone for about 10 to 15 minutes and I sure as hell didn't leave the window open.

"Hey, listen. You're right I, I got a lot of questions. This whole telepathy thing will take some getting used to," I laughed, nervously keeping an even kilter, non-aggressive tone. I walked slowly around my apartment peeping around and beneath every piece of furniture I owned. But I didn't see or hear anything. I looked around my bedroom expecting to find its red eyes glowing in a corner somewhere. But nothing.

I hurried over to the window and looked out. It was human out. The air had a peculiar, musty odor. I expected to see the large, Persian cat sitting in the moonlight licking its paws. But nothing. I heard no voice, no angry words or threats, just silence. I grabbed a chair from the kitchen table and turned it facing the window and waited. I sat there for two- hours before I stood up to stretch my legs. Unbelievably, after all the ducking and dodging I did, after all the denials and insanity checks, I really wanted the cat to come back.

The night passed into morning. I left my window open every day, occasionally, looking up and down the alleyway in back of my building. I went to work although I couldn't focus. Sometimes during lunch, I hurried back home to see if it had returned. But there wasn't even a clue that it had been there. Two weeks turned into a month-long anticipation. In reality, I had made the greatest discovery in humankind and just as quickly, had lost it. Most days I sit at my desk staring at the walls trying to figure out what it was all for. The human robot-like idiots I worked with didn't seem to mind the treadmill of their monotonous lives.

Evan, the annoying guy who sat at the desk next to me prior to my promotion, now had to catch me in the hallway or in the elevator. He was like the kid back in high school who never did his homework and cheated off everyone's paper.

"I haven't seen you around much since you've been hanging out with the boss's daughter," he sneered.

"What is it, Evan?" I sighed.

"I need a jingle for a funeral home, and I'm stuck. It's for a national radio campaign," he answered.

"Funeral homes can be tricky. First, take a step back and ask yourself what if it was my family member who died? What would it take for me to call this funeral Home?"

"That makes sense," he stared at the elevator doors.

"Play off of this: **We treat your family like one of our own!**" I said. But I didn't see why it was so hard for him to come up with.

"Holy shit!" He frowned. "That's it. That's fucking good. I can build off that. Thanks, Jack. Thanks, you saved my ass again," he hugged me.

Dude was just way too emotional. When the elevator doors opened on my floor, I had to pry him off to get out. "Next time I see you at Ray's, drinks are on me," he yelled excitedly. I smiled and walked off.

All the unimaginable things that feline revealed to me about the universe stayed on my mind. Yet all the horrible things it did stayed on my mind as well. But it was just as much a victim of animal cruelty as a cat at the rescue shelter. Except its abusers came from millions of miles away. Through no fault of its own it was turned into an aggressive, little monster that I unfortunately stumbled across in the alleyway. For decades humans have claimed to be abducted by aliens, probed, tagged, and released. But no one ever considered the fact that animals were their first experiments. Were they now watching me because of the things that deranged cat exposed about them? Were they now going to abduct me, study me, torture me, or make me disappear like countless others?

We were told ridiculous things over and over again until we believed them. We were denied knowledge, real knowledge of how things work. I was completely confused about where I stood in the universe. Me, a tiny product of nothing in comparison to the vastness of it all. I wanted to see, hear, and experience what that incomparable feline told me about. All the things that I'd been taught as a child to be impossible, I found out was indeed possible.

We're constantly being lied to and taking advantage of. My life, my goals, my dreams had to be bigger. My motivation was the veil that had been lifted from my eyes. I'd been awakened by a hairy, dangerous feline and I had no intention of going back to sleep.

It Put What in Its Mouth?

Some days I felt like I was suffocating, drowning in a pool of fear and anxiety. It became increasingly harder for me to sleep. My doctor prescribed sleeping pills that rarely worked. And when they did kick in, I felt lethargic; having crazy nightmares that I couldn't remember when I woke up. So many lingering questions kept me up at night. Aliens were real and they walked amongst us-doing whatever they wanted to whomever they wanted. I wondered if the government knew. Or maybe all this time the politicians have been throwing us to the wolves to save their own lying necks; just to maintain power. I couldn't rest or relax knowing that all my happiness may be short lived. Something unstoppable could be waiting around the next corner. We'd be fools to assume they'd be friendly. After all, we were never friendly to each other. Would there be an invasion or mass abductions? I wondered what a UFO looked like on the inside. I wondered why they chose to experiment on animals. I couldn't get that dam cat or anything it told me out of my head.

I went to work because I had to eat and pay the bills. But my enthusiasm and drive had all but disappeared in a cloud of trepidation. My job, my promotion, my big plans for the future didn't seem like anything worth striving for. I used to think of my colleagues as mindless robots but now they were mindless sheep, an entire herd of fools grazing for money. They were clueless about the real world around them and who controlled it. I found myself at Ray's bar at least every other night, obnoxiously hitting on every skirt I saw. Sometimes I wouldn't leave until he closed, chasing out all the alcoholics and drunks who fell asleep at their tables. My detached attitude had turned into self-destructive behavior. Ray tried to help but I wasn't trying to hear him.

"Look man, that George Michael stubble may work in here, but I know you ain't going to work like that," he frowned.

"No, I took a few days off. I got some PTO to use up," I shrugged.

"And you're just going to spend your days off sitting in here?"

"What, why not?" I asked.

He pointed at the clock on the wall. "It's 1:30 a.m. and you and that fat guy with that tight ass shirt on, are always the last ones in here. I'm not trying to tell you what to do with your life, but you've been drinking and partying way too much, dude. What's gotten into you?" Ray stared at me in disbelief.

"Nothing, I'm cool," I answered in a muffled voice.

"You're cool, huh? Let me ask you something; did you take that brunette home with you last night?" He frowned.

"Yeah, so..." I shrugged.

"So?" He repeated as a sour expression appeared on his face. "Dude, she was ugly as hell. I wouldn't have fucked her with your dick," he replied.

"Beauty is in the eye of the beholder," I said cynically.

"Really! What about that girl in the wheelchair the other night. I saw you roll her out of here. Or...or that lady with the patch over her eye looking like a goddamn pirate?" Ray shook his head.

"What's your point?" I asked. "Are you my father now?"

"Your sex addiction is out of control. You need another hobby because having sex with a bunch of randoms ain't what's happening, man," Ray reprimanded me in his usual straightforward way.

He sounded like my father. But he wasn't much older than me. "Sex addiction? What sex addiction? Because I don't like going home alone?" I asked.

"You used to at least pick quality over quantity. Now it seems like you just don't give a fuck?" Ray threw up his hands dramatically.

"Honestly, for weeks now, I haven't been wanting to go home alone. I feel... I feel..."

"You feel what?" He asked. "You ain't heard no more of those voices, have you? I told you to ignore that shit, man. They're going to put you in a strait jacket if you don't," he warned.

"No, I haven't but I feel kind of paranoid. You know, ever since that cat disappeared, I feel like I'm being watched. You know?" I sighed. "Then one morning last week I got up for work and saw the window to the fire escape open. Nothing was missing but I sure as hell didn't leave it open."

Ray gave me an unusual stare as he rubbed his neatly manicured beard. His face had a look of serious concern. He yelled over to his bar-back. "Throw that guy out of here and lock the doors. I've got to holla at my man here about something. We're going to my office. Come on," he said.

I followed him into his office, and he shut the door. He then opened the bottom drawer to his desk and pulled out a fat bottle of Cognac and two glasses.

"Here!" He poured us both a healthy amount and I knew right away something was up.

"What's going on?" I asked.

"Do you remember the last time I was at your place?"

"Dude, I apologized for that. I was under a lot of pressure and..."

"No... no just listen," he gulped down his drink and poured himself another one. "When me and Toni left that night, we cut through the alley behind your building," he hesitated. "Well... sometimes Toni and me... we get a little freaky and... you know, we kind of... do it outside. You know, the whole thrill of almost getting caught sort of thing. That's how we spice shit up," Ray loosened up his tie.

"Why didn't I think of that?" I laughed, but he didn't. He stared sternly at me, and I immediately wiped the grin off my face. "Sorry," I mumbled. Then I unintentionally giggled. "Mr. clean was having sex outside," I mumbled. The liquor made me say that.

Ray sighed and shook his head. "I said we like to spice things up. Now can you please shut the fuck up so I can finish?"

I nodded affirmatively.

"The whole time we were doing it, I felt uncomfortable; like we were being watched. And not in a good way, either. I looked up and there was something standing on the fire escape outside of your window. I could tell right away it was your window because of those ugly ass, puke green curtains your mama gave you."

I sat up in my chair and squirmed a bit. I realized his story wasn't going to be humorous at all. I could tell by his demeanor it was about to take an ominous turn. A troubled look appeared on his face.

"I thought I was drunk but the motherfucker was holding a big-ass, black cat; just like the Persian one you described. When me and that thing locked eyes, it was cold...weird..."

"Wait, what do you mean thing?" I asked.

"Honestly man, it looked like a goddamn monster...like a gray colored, giant anorexic ET or some shit, you know, like from the movie?" He asked.

"Yeah," I mumbled in astonishment. My lips barely moving. "Why in the hell didn't you tell me?" I asked hysterically.

"I thought I was drunk or high or... or just seeing things," he answered.

"But why are you telling me now?" I asked.

"That shit messed my head up man. I tried to block it out. Then you tell me your window was open," Ray tossed back another shot of cognac. "Because if it's real, then you've got a big fucking problem, I'd say."

"What do you mean?" I frowned.

"Well, it was holding that cat, rubbing it and stroking its fur with its long Frankenstein fingers. Then I heard a voice in my head as clear as you and me are talking right now. It said, "tell Jack I'm sorry." Then the alien thing opened its mouth, like four times the size of a normal mouth. It had teeth all around like a shark. It snapped the cat's neck, squeezed, and twisted it, then stuffed it into its mouth and started chewing," he stared down at the floor. "I can still hear its bones cracking."

"Jesus Christ," I bulked. That's why I hadn't seen that cat.

"Yeah, Jesus Christ is right. I threw up all over my old lady," he looked at me reflectively- shaking his head. "Then I grabbed her by the arm, without even zipping my zipper and we got the fuck out of there," said Ray.

I was speechless. All I could do is stare dumbfoundedly. "I can't believe you didn't tell me all this shit, man."

"No more than you could believe that cat was communicating with you, I didn't believe anything I saw or heard that night." Ray opened the same drawer he kept his favorite liquor and pulled out a black .38 revolver. "Keep this with you and move out of that apartment. Move in with one of them women you've been kicking it with. Because if your window was open, they're going in and out of your house," he warned.

Goddamn, why did he have to say that? I took a deep breath. "There were a couple of nights last week I got the Erie feeling I was being watched, you know. I stayed up a couple of nights looking at TV until it got light outside." I took a deep breath. My heart was pounding. "But what good is this gun going to be?" I asked.

"I don't know. It's better than nothing," answered Ray.

"Look, I've got to go!" I stood up and huffed. I felt confused. I was nervous. Now, I knew why the cat never came back. It was dead; eaten alive by its hideous former master.

"Go where? What are you going to do?" He asked.

"I don't know," I shrugged. "I honestly don't know."

Pillow Talk

"Hello, Jen?"

"Hey Jack? What is it that you want?" She said in a sarcastic voice that didn't sound happy to hear from me.

"Something wrong?" I asked."

"I haven't talked to you in weeks. And it seems I only hear from you when you want sex. Or someone to vent to. So, what do you want?" She replied.

Okay, here we go. "No... no... no... it's not like that." But it was. "I've been busy. That's all?"

"Too busy to answer a freaking text?"

Sure, I ignored her text. Because I could tell she was getting emotional. I didn't want a relationship and that's what our pillow talk had led to. She was catching feelings. I've been there before. Women are sentimental creatures when it comes to sex. Men are able to separate sex from emotion. But women have so many intricate lady parts, up top and down below, that it gets all tangled up and shit.

Sure, Jen was different. We connected sexually, but she was also intelligent, hardworking, fun-loving, with no children. I knew that if we saw too much of each other, I'd eventually be trapped into leaving my toothbrush and shaving gear over her house. Then comes a couple pairs of underwear and socks. And let's not forget her all female regiment of products cluttering up my own bathroom.

"Yeah, I had a lot going on at work with my promotion and all. I felt like I was drowning. I'm sorry for the miscommunication," I said softly.

"You know I like you Jack, I do, but..."

"I just want you to come over this weekend. And spend some time with me, that's all?" I blurted out.

"Oh, really!" she said sarcastically again.

"Yeah, we don't even have to do anything. I just want to see you," I said reassuringly. But even while the words were coming out of my mouth, **Stiff John** jumped up as if I had called his name.

Jen was quiet for a few seconds and then, "okay, I don't have anything planned. But I'm not going to start dropping everything because you, all of a sudden, have the urge to see me. That's not how things are going to work."

"No, not at all," I replied.

"I'll see you around 6:00 or 6:30," she said and hung up.

I felt relieved. Thank God! I did need her. I needed company. I didn't want to be alone. It seemed like every time I was home alone something strange or unusual was happening. The description of the thing outside my window had me paranoid. How many times has it been back? Had it been in my bedroom? Maybe standing over me as I slept? I thought about that cat. Ray said the alien ate him like he was nothing more than a sandwich. Even after all the horrible things it did, in a weird way, I kind of felt sorry for it.

"Tell Jack I'm sorry" were its last words. Wow, it had been used and disposed of like garbage. Ray was right, I did have to move. But until I did, I wasn't going to stay home alone. I put the gun under my pillow and waited for Jen to arrive.

"I brought my toothbrush and a couple of other things. But please don't panic," she smiled.

"See, was that necessary?" I laughed.

"I know how you men are, especially you confirmed bachelors. You get nervous when a woman leaves something over your house. You get really skittish," she laughed.

"There you go again," I smirked. But she was right. Maybe I wanted my cake and eat it too. But I still gave her a big hug, better than the last time I saw her. I wanted to show how much I appreciated her coming over for the weekend. I felt calmer, more relaxed.

On a Friday night like this, you normally would've found me out-and-about, bar hopping and partying. And then inevitably ending up at Ray's, eating wings and talking shit to the ladies. But since Jen was over, I stayed home. You can't take sand to the beach. Although under normal circumstances I would've tried. But I was feeling really bummed out about everything that had been going on. Jen brought a bottle of imported wine. Women love wine and Netflix. It would be more accurate to say she watched television while television was watching me. I had my own movies going on in my head, colorful, vivid, and frightening. But Jen seemed to be enjoying herself and I was glad. She sipped her wine while occasionally staring up at me with a curious smile. I guess she could sense the distraction in my eyes. She took my hand.

"Come on, let's sit outside," she grinned.

We climbed out onto the fire escape. I was surprised to see it wasn't as humid as I thought it would be. I didn't want to perspire all over my weekend guest. Jen fastened my arms around her waist. It was a romantic gesture to get me aroused. She pressed her butt up against my crotch, teasing my dick with her soft round ass. But me and **Stiff John** didn't move. I stared hypnotically down the alleyway, asking myself, what if. I couldn't help but wonder if we were standing in the exact same spot where the alien devoured that menacing cat. I looked down for trickles of blood spatter. I also searched the sky for unusual lights or flying objects. I couldn't help it.

"Hello," Jen said softly.

I squeezed her, then kissed her neck.

"Are you going to tell me what's going on?"

"What?" I replied.

"I've been here for hours, and you haven't tried to jump my bones once." She reached down and grabbed a handful of my loins. "See, you're not even getting hard."

"I guess I've got a lot on my mind, sorry!"

"Well.... sir, you know you can talk to me," she said reassuringly.

I hesitated. Other than Ray, no one else knew what was going on. Or what I'd been through. "You're going to think I'm a nut Job and never spend the night with me again," I replied.

She took a deep breath. "I don't know about that. A girl can overlook a lot of craziness when a man is giving her multiple orgasms," she laughed. And that made me laugh. I was starting to relax.

"If you promise not to call my parents and get them all worked up. My mom would try to make me move back to Jersey."

"So, your mama's boy?" She giggled.

"Sometimes. But my dad likes to walk around the house butt naked. So, he doesn't want me back there," I laughed. Then there was an awkward silence. I didn't know where to begin. But I told her. I started with the cat in the alley. She'd already seen the large, hairy cat with the red eyes. So, I told her about the voices I was hearing. I told her about the dude getting attacked and bitten. I told her what Ray said he'd seen while standing in the exact same spot.

"Wow!" She said softly. "That was a lot to unload on a girl." I was waiting for her to be dismissive, but she wasn't. "I knew there was something off kilter about that cat. Its energy was way, way too wicked," she said.

"Wait, so you believe me?" I asked.

"Why shouldn't I? You aren't making this up, are you?"

"No, of course not. It's just that, it's so unbelievable and..."

"I've studied a lot of things in my life, Jack. And unexplained phenomenon has always intrigued me." She must have sensed I was uneasy. She slid her hands around my back and into my pockets to make me feel comfortable again. "I'm currently taking a course in paranormal studies. They teach us to investigate crimes of paranormal phenomena and we conduct our own independent studies, projects, and paranormal investigations. So, this is right up my alley," she sighed. "The first thing they taught us is not to doubt anything you see or hear until it's been properly investigated enough to be disproved."

"So, you really believe me, huh?" I was surprised.

"You show no signs of mental illness. Your bachelor pad is neat, but not obsessively clean. Your job is stable, and you aspire for promotions and workplace status. Sure, you party like a frat boy but you're young. I'd say, yes, you're very credible."

"Damn, you should be a teacher or something. A sexy teacher," I smiled. I didn't realize how much of a turn on intelligence could be. **Stiff John** noticed it too.

"Oh, so now you're awake," she said softly, pressing her butt against my erection.

"Why don't we finish talking about this in my bedroom?" I said as we hurried back inside. I shut and locked the window and made sure I left every light on in the house, too.

After Jen fell asleep, I was up staring at the ceiling. I kept thinking about the night I crawled in here drunk. It was something that cat said that got the wheels in my head turning.

"It's a spacecraft in the woods in Connecticut. People think those woods are haunted. It's not, it's them."

I pulled out my laptop and began searching for information about hunted forests in Connecticut. And there it was. The words jumped out at me like flashing lights on a highway.

Haunted.... Dark Entry Forest.... Closed to the public.... Disappearances... Suicides... Strange sightings.... Do not enter....

I was seriously creeped out, but I was also intrigued. Was I the only person who knew what was really going on? I couldn't understand why that feline menace decided to confide in me. I didn't feel lucky. I felt confused. But now, its last words were stuck in my head like an earworm. What was I going to do about it? Do I call the police or some government agency? I already knew they wouldn't believe me.

I continued scrolling. My fingers pressing the keyboard like a piano, gathering as much information as I could. That's when I came across an interesting video on YouTube. There were these two guys, dressed in fatigues holding rifles and displaying large Bowie knives, saying how they were going to get to the bottom of things. They were going to find out where and why all the people who went into those woods in Connecticut ended up missing. They asked an important question too; was the government involved in this cover-up? They seemed really pissed off. When they rotated the camera, they were surrounded by other people who were upset and outraged, dressed in camouflage with their faces covered. They were all going to make the journey into Dark Entry Forest to find answers.

I became anxious as I sat up in bed. Then I had an epiphany; an idea I could commit to. I sat on the edge of my bed. Before long, I was quietly pacing my bedroom floor. A flurry of thoughts, ideas, and scenarios were flooding my head. I wanted to be one of those people. I wanted to find out for myself what was going on. I could do what that cat intended; expose these experiments; expose the covert invasion. And if the aliens were in fact coming in and out of my apartment, I wasn't going to be here. Me and those crazy YouTube motherfuckers were going to be in their back yard. I was going to embark on the adventure of a lifetime. Facing my fears would be the only way I'd find solace or closure.

I woke up to the smell of bacon and eggs filling my nostrils and forcing my stomach to growl. Aside from my mother it had been years since a woman had made breakfast in my kitchen. Jen was full of fun surprises. She was smart, intelligent, sexy, knew how to party and she could cook. That's when a strange thought jumped into my head. Maybe it wouldn't be so bad seeing her underwear and toothbrush in my bathroom every day. No, I had to admonish those kinds of thoughts. They were the restricting thoughts of a man looking to be tied up and tied down. That sure as hell wasn't me. Besides, I had bigger fish to fry. I didn't need an emotional attachment clouding my judgment.

"Hey you!" I snuck up and kissed her on the cheek. She was wearing one of my t-shirts that barely covered her ass. And she didn't have on any panties either. "Smells good."

"Thanks!" She smiled."

As I sat at the table savoring every delicious mouthful, Jen noticed I gulped down my orange juice and immediately got up to refill my glass. Is this what it would be like to be in a relationship with her? Or was this whole, delicious breakfast-thing designed to reel me in? Was great sex, good food, stimulating conversation and attentiveness to my needs, all part of Jen's master plan to bait me into an exclusive relationship? I didn't know. But hell, it was working.

"What are you staring at?" She asked."

I didn't realize I was staring. "You look good without makeup," I answered.

"What?" She frowned.

"I mean, you know, some women don't look so good in the morning, especially not wearing makeup. But you look...rather good," I replied. And **Stiff John** was thinking the exact same thing.

"Hummmm!" She squinted. "Are you okay?"

"Yeah, I'm good," I smiled.

"Do you want some more pancakes or eggs? She asked. "I cooked plenty."

"That's not what I want to eat right now." I stood up and stepped over to her side of the table. I pulled her chair slightly backwards before lifting her onto the marble countertop. I raised her shirt up to her neck and kissed her shapely breasts. I licked my way down to her belly button and then to her opening.

"Oh Jack," she panted softly. "You're so nasty...and I love it."

A couple of hours later Ray stopped by. I told him I had something important to tell him that I couldn't discuss over the phone. He didn't seem too thrilled to hear my big news.

"Are you high right now, man? This shit sounds crazy as hell. Have you ever been to Connecticut? Have you ever slept out in the woods? Have you..."

"Hey, calm down, dude. I went hunting with my dad when I was a kid. I know what I'm doing. Besides, I'm determined to see this thing through."

Jen walked into the living room.

"Is this your new girlfriend?" Asked Ray.

"No!" We both answered at the same time.

"We're just friends," Jen smirked.

"This is my buddy, Ray." They both shook hands.

"Did you know your friend here plans on going to Connecticut to hunt for UFO's?" Asked Ray.

"He told me a few minutes before you got here," replied Jen. She held up her iPhone. "It says a lot of people disappear in that forest."

I looked at Jen. "It was kind of your idea," I shrugged.

"What!" She and Ray both blurted out at the same time.

"I said no such thing," frowned Jen.

"No, you told me these things were worth investigating."

"But that didn't mean run off half- cocked to Connecticut," she said. "It could be dangerous!"

"Look, check this out." I pulled up the video of the team of guys I was going to be working with. I was actually kind of excited too.

Ray looked over at Jen, then back at me. "Dude, you're seriously going to go into the woods with those country ass hillbillies; redneck looking motherfuckers?"

I showed him the emails and the correspondence I had with the one named Roland. "They're a bunch of tough, heavily armed, paramilitary guys." I answered. "They were in Afghanistan and Iraq just like you."

"Yeah, well everybody seems tough until shit hits the fan. If you ask me, it looks like the movie 'Deliverance' just waiting to happen. And guess what? You ain't Burt Reynolds." He poked me in the chest.

"Deliverance?" I asked. "What the hell is that?"

Jen Frowned. She obviously knew what he was talking about, but I didn't. "You don't want to know," she sighed.

"You know what Ray, extraterrestrials aren't watching you or going in and out of your house," I pointed out.

"You're being visited by aliens?" Jen looked nervously around the apartment.

"I take it Jack's told you everything, huh?" Ray stared at me like it was supposed to be a secret.

Jen gave an expressionless nod. "It's some really bizarre things happening but..."

"Look, I just wanted to let you both know what was going on in case I encounter any problems, that's all. Now, I've got to start getting ready. So..." It was a three-hour drive and I wanted to get there before dark.

Ray knew it was pointless to badger me after I'd made up my mind about something. He always said it was because of my zodiac sign. He was into astrology, chanting, meditating and a bunch of other shit.

"Alright Taurus, text me once in a while to let me know how things are going, okay," Ray patted me on the shoulder.

"Of course," I smiled. "There's nothing to worry about, okay."

"I don't know what you're hoping to find out there, but good luck and watch your back," Ray shrugged. "Nice to meet you, Jen."

As soon as the door shut, I grabbed Jen and pulled her close to me, shoving my tongue into her mouth while fondling her breasts.

"You're an animal today," she mumbled as my tongue slid in and out of her mouth. "You want more already?"

I didn't answer. I squeezed her tighter as I dominantly pushed my fingers down her jeans and inside her. "Is this going to be waiting for me when I get back?" I asked.

"If you want it to be," she said softly, trembling a bit. "Ah!" she grunted and grabbed my arm. "Stop, you're going to start something you can't finish. You said you were about to leave."

"I know but I wanted to take something with me along the way," I smiled.

Jen laughed and laid her head on my chest. My dad told me years ago, whenever you're going on a trip, the best energy you can take along is knowing someone was waiting for you when you got back home. It was as close to good luck as you were going to get. I packed my duffel bag and went to the car. After Jen left, I deliberately didn't wash my hands. I wanted her scent on me. I wanted to smell my fingers as I drove down the highway and into the unknown. It was to remind me that if I so desired, she would be mine permanently. So once in a while I would smell my fingers and reminisce. Maybe my bachelor days are over. I don't know. But I knew that having someone to come back to was important. I also knew that going into a place called Dark Entry Forest was a crazy idea. But if I was going to expose everything while at the same time finding closure, it was a risk I had to take.

Meeting the 'A' Team

It was little to no traffic once I left the city. Maybe that was a good sign; showing me the clear path I was meant to follow, explore, and expose. My mind kept drifting back to the things my unwelcome feline visitor told me. It said we weren't really safe. We were all in danger. I realized that if no one did anything, something bad was going to happen and soon. These extraterrestrials, these highly advanced beings have been doing whatever they pleased to all of us. We were their experiments; their toys to be pushed about like a child's playthings scattered across the floor. We were picked up, admired then eventually broken. They'd wind us up and take notes on how we destroy ourselves and each other. Who knows how long this game has been going on, decades, centuries?

I drove about three hours and Google Maps took me straight to the hotel door. We were to meet at an off the highway bread and breakfast called Cornwall Inn. It looked like a house someone had converted into a hotel. It wasn't the Marriott, but I wasn't there for luxury nor was I there to complain. I kicked back on the bed and watched old sitcoms to relax. I was nervous but I was also excited. I'd never been on any real adventure before in my life. And this was big by anyone's standards. I woke up at 5:00 a.m. and got myself together. I was outside the hotel standing next to my car doing a few leg stretches, when a pickup truck and a cargo van with dark, tinted windows pulled up next to me. Three guys and a woman stepped out of the van, while two guys jumped out of the truck. They all walked up to me and stared.

"You Jack?" The muscular man asked. It was the guy from the video. "I'm Roland."

We shook hands. "Yeah, I'm Jack."

"That's what I figured," said Roland. "And I'm glad you're on time. I like that," he nodded. "Anyway, this is my wife Renae, and my brother Quinn. That's my man Matt. He's the gadgets guy on this mission. That tall gentleman over there is Preacher. He's got location and logistics. And that's Ethan with the camera."

I shook everybody's hand and watched as they tried to size me up, and vice versa.

"Dude, you don't look that old," said Ethan. He was wearing gold chains, rings and some expensive boots. I could tell because I almost bought the exact same pair before I came to my senses.

"I'm almost thirty," I lied. But thirty sounded better than twenty-five.

"That's what's up," he nodded. "Wait, you're not camera shy are you, dude?" Ethan asked. "Sometimes, I'm going to be live-streaming our search to my half-a-million followers."

"It's cool," I shrugged.

Ethan reminded me of a hip-hop wannabe. White, middle-class kids who immersed themselves in rap culture. He didn't seem to take our mission seriously. The rest of the team had profoundly serious demeaners.

But when I shook Roland's wife's hand she laughed. "I don't know about this one. His hands are softer than yours, Ethan. I bet he hasn't been camping since the boy scouts," they all laughed.

I just smiled and stared at her, briefly. I didn't respond to what could be considered an insult.

"Okay everybody, listen up," said Roland. "We've all got our own reasons for being here. But remember two things; one, this is serious business. And two, I'm in charge. People go missing in Dark Entry Forest a lot. And if you don't want to be one of them, do exactly what I tell you, when I tell you. Any questions?" There was silence. And I certainly wasn't about to raise my hand and ask any of my stupid questions. "Last, if anybody wants to change their mind and go home, now is the time."

Everyone was silent.

"Jack, leave your car here and ride with Preacher and Ethan. Our entry point is about two miles up the road. Check your gear and supplies on the way. Mount up!" He said authoritatively.

And here we were. A group of strangers and I were about to enter one of the most notorious forests in America. Suddenly, I felt a nervous tingle in my stomach. It was to be expected. But I wasn't worried. The group I was with seemed more than capable.

"So, dude, what's your story? I heard you were from New York. I'm from Long Island. We call that shit strong Island." Ethan pointed his handheld camera at me. "And Kim-Kong 87 thinks you're cute," he smiled.

He was live streaming, and I wasn't sure how to feel about being watched and scrutinized by a bunch of college kids and sci-fi junkies. It was obvious Ethan was a keyboard cowboy who decided to get from behind his computer and into the field.

"I've been hearing about this place, and I wanted to check it out. But I didn't want to go by myself," I answered. I sure as hell wasn't going to tell him or anyone else a conversation with an alley cat bought me here.

"Wise man," said Ethan. "Hey Preacher, tell Jack what happened to your arm."

I looked over the seat at the old man driving the truck. He was wearing a short-sleeved camouflage shirt. Aside from his old, weather-beaten tattoos, his arm looked fine to me. "What about his arm?" I asked, as the preacher kept his eye on the road.

"What are you, blind? His left arm is fake," said Ethan nonchalantly. He came off as insensitive.

"Oh damn," I quipped. "Sorry to hear that," I frowned. I don't know what made me say that.

"What are you sorry for?" Ethan laughed. "You didn't do it, did you?" Then he turned the camera on himself so that his viewers could see him laughing.

"Hey kid, do you ever shut the fuck-up?" Preacher stuck a cigarette into his mouth and lit it, all the while steering the truck with his knee.

"Yeah, when I'm sleep," he replied. "So, are you going to tell him?" Pestered Ethan.

The sixty-plus looking man gave Ethan a sour expression. He was clearly annoyed with the younger man's disrespect. But his distasteful glare didn't seem to faze Ethan at all. He kept the camera pointed at him.

"I'd been looking for UFO's most of my adult life, following leads and going wherever the information took me. Although I was a minister, I always felt there were things the Bible didn't tell us because they didn't know themselves. I'd been getting closer and closer to the truth about these aliens, and they knew it. People think they're aliens in Roswell, New Mexico but they ain't there. They moved everything to Wright-Patterson Air Force Base in Ohio, see. Long story short; about ten years ago me and a friend commandeered a jeep and two military-police uniforms. We snuck onto

Wright-Patterson's top-secret installation. After some maneuvering, we found ourselves in an underground bunker below hanger 18. We were knee deep in some real shit, man. We saw everything. They had aliens down there; dead and alive, a spaceship our scientists were reverse engineering, contaminated animals, crossbred livestock, you name it. We took pictures and a few top-secret files, too."

"See, folks think it's only one group of aliens but there ain't. There are at least five that frequent earth. And whenever they crash, their remains are hauled off and kept on ice and freezing water. Seen it with my own eyes. Everything gets swept under the rug, you know. A few days after we left the base, we were headed straight to the Washington Post Newspaper to expose everything. That Watergate guy Bob Woodward was expecting us too. Well, that night we was in the hotel room; my buddy Swoop was in his bed, me, in the one closest to the bathroom. I had a little bladder problem back then. Anyhow, the next morning when I wakes up, my buddy Swoop had gone missing. And I mean gone.... vanished. And so were the pictures and the files. His bed was made up like it had never been slept in. But I'd seen him get in it.

"And well," he looked down at his left shoulder, that wasn't the only thing missing. My arm was gone. I mean, it just won't there. At first, I thought I was dreaming. I started screaming and yelling and looking around the hotel room. When I looked in the mirror it won't nothing but a smooth, surgical scar. No pain, no swelling, nothing." He exhaled like a man reliving a nightmare. "I ran down into the lobby butt-ass naked. The police had to hold me down and strap me to a gurney.

"God damn!" I balked. What the hell? "How is something like that even possible?" I asked.

"I don't know. I didn't feel nothing. They must have used some kind of nerve gas. I called Swoops wife, his job, his mother, but nobody had seen him. I even filed a police report. It was like he dropped off the face of the earth. His wife, the police, everybody thought I had killed him. They investigated me for years. Hell, my own wife and daughter got a restraining order, and had me put in the nut house for months. They said I was a danger to myself and others." His face became contorted with anger. "You ever been in an overcrowded, underfunded, inner-city psych ward, kid?"

I shook my head 'no.'

"Well don't." He threw his cigarette butt out the window and quickly lit another one. "Nobody ever believed what I said happened. Imagine how that feels. And the shrinks said I must've hurt myself and got my arm amputated under an assumed name. Yeah right," he sneered. "But I ain't never stopped looking for Swoop. I figure he'd do the same for me."

"Why in the hell did they do that?" I asked. I believed every word he said. He was credible but I was more scared than curious.

"Well, we're talking about the Grays. The coldest, most diabolical, unfeeling species to set foot on this planet. I mean, why do we pull the legs off June bugs and frogs? Or experiment on lab rats? Because that's what we are to them, a bunch of human lab rats. They didn't want to kill me. They wanted to slow me down and send a message."

"At least they didn't cut off your dick," said Ethan. He didn't crack a smile either. The idiot was dead serious.

"Get that camera out my face! I don't feel like talking no more," Preacher sniffled a bit. I just hoped he wasn't about to cry. His story was so sad, I damn near wanted to cry.

Once we arrived at the designated area, ex-marine Sergeant Roland handed out weapons, hunting knives, rifles, smoke grenades and plenty of bullets.

"By now, you all know what happened to Preacher," Roland reached into a tote bag. He gave us gas masks with extra filters. "Thanks to him we know how diabolical these bastards can be. Wear these to bed every night or whenever you go to sleep. This is an expedition to find evidence and show it to the public. We're not here to engage or confront the enemy, only to prove to the world that the enemy, does in fact, exist."

And then, we walked single file into the thick patch of grassy marshland and trees; trees that looked like they formed a doorway all of their own. We walked bravely into Dead Entry Forest. The place of no return.

Welcome to the Unknown

Roland looked down at his watch. "All right, let's take ten," he ordered. He was a confident guy. If he didn't know where we were going, he sure acted like he did. I popped open my canteen of water. The landscape was rocky and steep in some places, but the low-lying areas were like mash pits; muddy, wet, and humid. We had literally walked four miles non-stop, and I was tired.

"You doing a lot of sweating city boy. You alright?" Roland's wife Renae laughed and nudged her brother-in-law, Quinn. He smiled a bit as he repeatedly wiped down his rifle. Renae was attractive. I could tell from the strings extending from beneath her blue bandana that her hair was naturally blonde. And she was fit too. I figured she and her ex-military husband worked out together. They reminded me of a couple of gym rats that could easily subdue me with a headlock.

After a few more miles, Roland found a spot for us to bed down for the night. We gathered wood and lit four small fires and laid down next to them. Roland said that our alien enemies probably had infrared vision. And with glowing fires it would be harder for them to detect how many of us there were. It made since. This guy was good.

"So, Jack, my viewers want to know; what made a shirt and tie guy like you run off into the wilderness with a bunch of crazies you saw on the internet?" Ethan's question was legit but the way he phrased things made him easy to dislike.

"I had a bad experience and I needed to prove something to myself, I guess. What about you?" I asked.

"Well, I wanted some real live content for my channel. Plus, I'm hoping I'll get a chance to shoot my guns off." He held his camera down to his waist to reveal two semi-automatic .45 caliber pistols he had on each hip. "People want to know if you've ever seen an alien. I mean, other than the ones who run across the border?" He laughed.

I saw Matt the tech Guy whisper something to Roland. The Sergeant stopped setting up the perimeter and walked over to us. "All right guys, listen up. Everybody put your phones on silent. Also, turn your resolution down to almost zero. We don't need flashing lights or your weird ass ringtones going off out here." He stared at Ethan with a disgusted look. "I told you before about that gold chain around your neck. It's like a goddamn reflector. Take it off and put it into your pocket."

"Dude, calm down. It's not that serious," replied Ethan.

"You're not going to fuck this up for us. The van is less than ten miles that way," Roland pointed. And I'll send your ass packing. I don't care how much money you've spent. Understand?" He asked.

Ethan stubbornly removed his rings, thick gold cross, diamond earrings and slid them into his jeans. I waited until Roland walked off before I asked Ethan what he meant by 'how much money he spent.' He turned his camera off and stared at me.

"Who do you think paid for all this fancy equipment? Me! This is all state-of-the-art technology, man. Over $15,000 worth of sensors, cameras, thermal imaging software, night vision, guns with scopes and lasers. Even those knives are $100 a pop," he said.

"That's cool, dude," I nodded.

"It's not cool. It's what had to be done. Besides, my dad's rich. That's this week's allowance for me. So, Mr. G.I. Joe over there needs to take a chill pill." He kicked his sleeping bag open and laid down next to the fire.

It was our first night sleeping in Dark Entry Forest and it was eerie. The normal sounds of nature seem to have vanished, replaced by a deafening quiet. There were no birds chirping, noisy crickets or even owls making those weird ass noises. It was just dead silence. If not for the crackle from the fires, there wouldn't be any noise at all. We'd hiked about 10 miles and according to Roland, an estimated five more to go. So far, so good.

I strapped my gas mask on and yanked it up and down to make sure it was properly sealed. Preacher's story had made me uneasy. I didn't want to wake up with none of my body parts missing, so I aligned my sleeping bag with Matt, the gadgets guy, who had strategically placed alarms and sensors around the entire campsite. As I laid there staring up at the stars, I couldn't help but wonder what other planets would look like up close. If there was somebody just like me staring into the night sky asking questions. The only thing I knew for sure was that we weren't alone. And that got me thinking about probabilities. What's the probability of our mission being a success? What would be the probability of us being able to prove to the world that aliens existed? But mainly, I kept trying to figure out why they didn't reveal themselves? Why were these aliens so elusive? And why were these Grays so ruthless? We posed no threat to them, but they roam our planet in secrecy and scare the fuck out of everyone. Why wouldn't they help us solve some of the world's problems? Was there something about us that scared them?

The next day after the formalities of morning greetings and who slept well and who didn't, we were on our way. I was on the didn't sleep well list. I kept thinking I was going to wake up missing my hands or feet or worse. I ended up staring into the forest all night. As we walked along at our single file pace, I somehow ended up in line in front of Renae. I looked back at her a couple of times. I couldn't help it. Her breasts were huge, and I kept wondering if they were real. I bet that retired Marine Corps guy has a good time with those things. What was I doing? Jesus Christ, I had to focus.

"Hey Roland, I think city boy here needs a break. Can we take Ten?" She asked her tireless husband. He seemed to never run out of energy.

"Yeah," he frowned.

I could tell he didn't want to stop. And why was Renae fucking with me? Maybe she caught me checking out her breasts. It didn't matter. I was kind of tired anyway. Roland's brother Quinn stood next to me watching the tree line with eagle eyes. He was also watching our backs. His brother was built like a refrigerator. However, Quinn was leaner but fit, nonetheless. Dude looked just as intimidating as his brother in his green hat, sunglasses and camouflage outfit. It reminded me of those mercenaries you see in movies. He was the definition of the strong, silent type. Even after standing guard most of the night, he was still super alert and ready.

Gadget guy walked up and handed me a tiny tracker. "Here, put this inside your sock. In case you get separated from the group, we'll be able to find you," he said.

"Dude, my followers think you look like Joe Rogan." Ethan put his fancy internet camera in Matt's face.

"Who?" He asked.

"You know, the Fear Factor guy," replied Ethan grinning.

"Sorry, I don't watch much tv," he shrugged. "You still got your tracker, right?" He asked.

"Yep, it keeps rubbing against my ankle," said Ethan.

"Unfortunately, that's the best place for it. Even if you lose your shoes more than likely, you'll still have your socks on."

Ethan seemed to never shut up. The guy was obsessed with recording everything. I know documenting our journey was important, but Ethan was more interested in clicks, likes, and views than the mission we were on.

Roland walked over to us. "Is your signal still strong?"

Ethan nodded.

"Good. Let's get back to it. In approximately two-hours we'll be at our rendezvous point," said Roland.

"What's that?" I asked.

"I have two associate's meeting us half-a-mile from where we believe the alien craft is located. They came from the opposite side of the mountain yesterday," said Roland.

"Damn, that's cool," I mumbled. I was super excited. We were almost there. We had reinforcements and one hell of a team leader, who seems to have thought of everything. Time moved quickly and it wasn't long before Roland was dictating orders to us again.

"Alright team, listen up. According to the signal we're about half-hour away from my rendezvous point. This is a perfect spot for base camp. Two of you are going to stay here for prep duty. The rest of us are moving forward. Quinn, Matt, Ethan, and Preacher are with me. Renae, you and Jack stay here and start setting up camp."

"Wait, why do I have to babysit city boy? I want to see what's on the other side of the mountain, too." She complained. Matt and Ethan laughed.

"No one's babysitting. This is a team and we've each got a position to play," Roland said sternly as he walked up close to his wife. He touched her shoulder, leaned in, and whispered something in her ear. I thought he was going to kiss her, but I guess he didn't want to appear weak or sensitive in front of the guys. "Set your radio to channel 22 and make sure your two- way is fully charged," he told her.

"Well, this is it," said Ethan. He fanned his internet camera around at all of us. He smiled at his viewers, but I could tell there was a sense of fear in his eyes. It was a fear of the unknown and the unexplained, both about to intersect on the other side of that mountain. He gave me a fist bump then ran to catch up with the other four men. Sometimes, he didn't seem so bad.

I kind of wanted to go but kind of didn't.

Renae dropped her backpack and began setting up a perimeter. "Jack, start getting the firewood and stay where I can see you."

"Okay," I answered. I had no problem taking orders from a woman. Renae had far more experience at being a survivalist than me. This was my first adventure and so far, so good. In the quietness of our surroundings, I began to think about ways to move forward and put this whole UFO thing behind me when this trip was over. This journey was about closure. I didn't want to end up like preacher spending a decade of my life searching for something I couldn't find and prove. I had to put that whole wicked ally-cat episode behind me. Today was going to be it. Once the others got back with pictures and video and other evidence, I was going to push my life in another direction. Come hell or high water this was going to be my closure.

I went a few feet outside the perimeter to take a leak. I didn't want to piss all over the ground where someone might be tossing their sleeping bag later. As I unzipped my pants, I still felt a bit uneasy about how quiet it was out here. The old adage about "does a tree make a sound in a forest when it falls, if there's no one around to hear it" popped into my head. I laughed. It's funny the things guys think about when we're taking a leak. But I needed to focus and stay alert. As soon as I had a nice, steady stream of water flowing someone touched my shoulder.

"Jesus Christ!" I jumped.

"Careful, you're going to get yourself all wet, Jack." Renae's voice was soothing, and her lips were unusually close to my ear. "I told you to stay where I could see you."

Did she just call me Jack instead of city boy? "I was just taking a…"

"Shhhh…!" She whispered softly as her other hand reached around my waist. Her breasts were now planted firmly against my back. Why was she so close? She moved my hand away from my shaft, as I offered no resistance, and replaced it with her own. She held and guided **Stiff John** as I wet the tree bark, the leaves, and the ground around it. Her soft cheek rubbed against my face and her feminine smell disarmed me. She swirled my dick around in circles like we men often do when we pee outside, even shaking the residual drips that could stain my underwear.

"There you go. All done, right?"

She kissed me on the neck and behind my ear, before putting my dick back into my underwear and zipping up my pants. Of course, I no longer had to piss hard. I had a hard- hard.

"Come on let's get back to work," she said walking away like she didn't just have her hand down my pants… like she didn't just help me urinate... as if I was a toddler... like her hand wasn't all over my dick. What the fuck just happened?

The team had been gone for hours. And soon it would be dark out. Renae and I had long since finished setting up camp, complete with battery-powered sensors and trip lines. We didn't use tents unless it was raining because Roland said they would obstruct our view. And he was right. Every movie I'd seen with people sleeping in a tent, they always got fucked up first. Renae was reading some kind of romance novel, while I scrolled up and down my social media. I was still surprised we actually got a signal this far in the woods.

"Um, hey Renae, can I ask you something?"

"Sure Jack, what is it?" She removed her bandana and brushed her blonde hair to one side.

"They've been gone a while. Is everything okay?"

"I just spoke to my husband on the two-way. They're just waiting for our associates to arrive. Nothing to worry about," she answered.

"Cool!" I nodded. But I kept staring at her, sitting there with her legs crossed, wearing camouflage stretch pants that I wished I could pull down and take a look. I was confused. Should I make a move on this sexy, married woman and risk being left in these woods by myself- if her husband found out? Or was what happened a couple of hours ago, just some weird thing she liked to do? I already knew what **Stiff John** wanted and now I was starting to see things his way. I was unknowingly staring at her.

"Is there something else, Jack?" She asked.

"Oh, yeah. I... I thought you didn't like me."

Renae smiled mischievously. "You have a lot to learn about women. A woman, especially a married one, will often pretend like she doesn't like a guy in order to throw her husband or boyfriend off the trail."

"Oh," I mumbled. "So, we have a connection?" I asked.

"Um, no. But you're so cute. I wanted to see what you were working with, that's all. And if you're nice, you may get an even better treat when this is over," she smiled again.

"Last question, I swear. What made you guys go searching for UFO's, aliens, and shit? I mean, it's not something regular people do?"

"In case you haven't noticed yet, we're not regular people. Then again, what is regular?" She laughed. "Roland, his brother and me were paid to protect this hot shot mayor who'd been talking shit about how he was going to fight corruption and clean up the city. He was exposing his colleagues and city officials who were taking payoffs and were in bed with underworld figures. A week before he was to testify to a grand jury, we took him to a school about three blocks from the courthouse so we wouldn't have far to go. The school was closed for the summer, so we knew no one was going to be there. We had the whole building to ourselves. We had plenty of provisions and a fat check waiting on us when we finished.

We were held up in the locker room with one way in and one way out. Then one night Roland came into the hallway to smoke a cig. The mayor had asthma so we all just smoked in the hallway. When he went back inside the mayor was gone. I mean, it's like he just disappeared into thin air. We searched that school for hours and nothing. It was the creepiest thing I ever experienced. We found burn marks in the ceiling but no mayor. Needless to say, his family as well as our employers thought we ghosted the guy. You know, sold him out to the ops. It fucked up our reputation and made Roland super depressed, you know?"

"That's crazy," I sighed.

"Yeah, well after a couple of days, other townspeople, a housewife and a mail carrier all disappeared too. Their families swore it was UFO's and we began to research it. We theorized the mayor must have been abducted by aliens as well. I mean, we ruled out all other possible scenarios."

"But what did they want with the mayor?" I asked.

"Well, I don't think it was because he was the mayor. I think The Grays tag people and watch or follow their lives with tracking devices. Just like we tag and track dolphins, white gorillas, Wales; they tag us."

"Goddamn! This rabbit hole just gets deeper and deeper," I sighed.

"Ain't that the truth," Renae agreed.

"Why are we here. I mean, it's like a dead forest. And we ain't seen nothing crazy yet?" I asked.

"A friend of Roland's kept getting pings from his homemade sonar whenever he's flying over this area. Then he saw heat signatures that he said were off.

"Off?" I frowned.

"Yeah, nothing is supposed to be out here. His readings would go red whenever he flew over this area. Then there was that naked girl the Park Rangers found not far from where we parked our vehicles. She had no memory of how she got there and barely remembered her damn name. So, we figured this may be one of their hideouts." Renae looked down. She could hear my phone vibrating in my pocket. "You need to put that on silent, Jack."

"I will." I looked down at my call log. "It's my buddy Ray. I'm going to answer it."

"Ray, what's going on, dude?" I was glad to hear from him. "I'm going to put you on facetime," I smiled. I had planned to call him earlier. I wanted him to see our camp.

"What's good with you, Jack?" He asked. He was wearing a white shirt, black tie, and jacket. I heard music in the background.

I knew he was at the bar. "How's the alien hunting going," he said sarcastically.

"So far, so good. We haven't found anything. And I'll probably be headed back that way tomorrow."

"Who's that behind you?" Ray squinted.

"That's Renae." I held my phone up so that he could see her better.

"Hello Renae!" Ray waved.

"Well now, caramel wrapped in a suit," she winked playfully.

"Oh...kay," a surprised Ray smiled politely.

"I'm just kidding," Renae laughed. "I'll leave you two alone," she chuckled.

"Is she gone?" He asked.

I put the phone close to my face. "Yeah, I laughed. " That's the team leader's wife. She carries a shotgun and AR-15," I said.

"Cool," Ray nodded. "Where's everybody else?"

"They went on ahead to take pictures and meet up with some other people. We're setting up camp," I answered.

"Just you and that chick are there alone?" Asked Ray.

I nodded my head 'yes'. I already knew why he asked that.

"Stay away from her Jack. You're not in a safe environment to be messing with some crazy ex-jarhead's wife."

"Funny you should say that because..."

Ray stopped me mid-sentence. "I don't want to know," he frowned.

Renae walked back over. "Okay gentleman, I hate to break up your male bonding, but Jack has chores to do," she yawned.

"Why are you yawning? Didn't you get enough sleep?" I asked.

"I guess not. You know these gas masks are uncomfortable in the first place. Then I kept having these weird dreams that someone was talking to me, telling me how they were going to kill me and eat me," she laughed. "And not eat me in a good way either."

"What, you had a dream about Hannibal Lecter?" I asked.

"You know how sometimes you're half awake and half asleep and you're like, still groggy. Well, it was as if someone was talking to me, but no one was there. Roland was asleep and this deep voice kept taunting me. Telling me how it was going to destroy all of us," said Renae.

I looked down at my phone. Rae and I both stared at each other with blank expressions on our faces.

"What? What's wrong?" Asked Renae.

"Jack..."

"I know," I said.

"Dude, you got to get the fuck out of there right now. Radio your team and tell them to get back to camp double-time."

"We will do no such thing. What's wrong with you two?" Asked Renae.

I had to tell her. This was too important to hide.

"I didn't tell you what brought me out here in the first place," I sighed. "A while back, I was on my way home and I found a stray cat in the alleyway. To make a long story short, I took it home and the next day, the damn thing started talking to me." I looked up at her face. She was trying hard not to laugh. I knew that was coming. "When I say talk, I mean not with an actual voice from the mouth but using some kind of telepathy."

Renee looked down at my phone and saw that Ray's face was deadly serious, as well. "You two have obviously been popping the same pills, geez. More evidence that all the really cute guys are crazy."

"No, listen to him, lady." Ray shouted through the phone.

"This.... this fucking cat told me that it was abducted, and the aliens did experiments on it, which resulted in him being able to communicate with humans. This cat was fucking vicious and blood-thirsty. It attacked people and other animals and loved the damage that it did."

"Give her the phone," said Ray. Renae took my phone and stared at Ray's solemn expression. "I didn't believe him either. Then one night I went by his apartment and outside his window, on his balcony, I saw a goddamn alien holding a black, Persian cat, with red eyes. And then it killed it."

"Jesus Christ, let's say I believe you. A talking cat, okay. So what," she asked.

I took my phone back. "It means it's something else out here in these woods, watching us. And it was communicating with you last night," I replied. "And why wouldn't you believe me?" I asked. "You said out of your own mouth that a guy you will protecting disappeared from a room with no windows, or no doors, and under heavy guard."

Renee took a deep breath and stared at me as she contemplated what I was saying.

"Do you really think humans are the only things these alien fuckers abduct and experiment on? You don't think they're sticking probes up animals' asses too?" I asked. "And these woods are just too quiet. No birds, no bugs, no crickets, no animals, nothing is out here. It's just too fucking weird."

"Then why are the phones still working," she asked.

"I don't know. Maybe it's just part of a game. These aliens love watching and taunting us. I don't know," I shrugged.

"Okay... Okay... I'll radio Roland and warn him," Renae sighed. She grabbed her long gun out of a tote bag. "You ever used an AR-15 City boy?" She asked.

"No," I mumbled.

"I'm going to show you. Tell your buddy you'll call him back," she said.

"Ray, I've got to go, I..."

"Good!" he exclaimed. He already knew what was up.

My heart began to beat faster. And I was afraid. "Hey, tell my parents I love them. And if you see Jen, tell her..." At that moment, my FaceTime call with Ray became fuzzy, cloudy, and then turned off all together. 'No Signal' popped up on the screen. An airplane appeared overhead. It was flying kind of low and spraying what looked like red paint from its rear.

"Finally," said Renae.

"What's going on?" I asked.

"Roland's business associate Wayne is spraying red dye over the area we think the alien craft is hiding. And since they've probably got some kind of cloaking device, it's going to show us exactly where it is?" She smiled.

Damn! That was smart, I thought.

Renae's walkie-talkie made a small chirping sound. "I was just about to call you," she said. "Is everything alright?"

"You're not going to believe this baby, but there's a long round structure just south of the clearing, hovering just below the tree line," said Roland. "Matt and Ethan were taking all kinds of videos, pictures and had started a live stream until they lost signal. Crazy right?" He sounded excited. "Well, we did it. We got what we came for. That red spray was genius if I may say so myself.... Copy."

"Copy that," Renae smiled. "So, listen, City boy Jack says there may be some kind of animal in the woods; vicious, possibly deadly, copy?"

"Ten-four. Tell 'em thanks. We're going on red alert," he replied. "See, this is going to be a big 'fuck-you' to everyone who thought I was crazy." The ex-marine's deep voice echoed.

"If you were crazy then all of us were crazy," replied his wife.

"We're less than a hundred and fifty yards away from the craft. We've got the intel and we're about to head back. Copy?"

"Great, stay on mission honey!" Said Renae.

"Wait, the door of the craft is opening. I Repeat, the door of the alien spaceship is opening. Something big just jumped out. I can't make out what it is. But it's damn fast. I don't like it. You two break camp, leave non-essentials, and head to the rally point. We'll meet you there. Copy?" Asked Roland.

"Copy!" Renae frowned as a look of concern appeared on her face. "You heard him. Grab your essentials and let's go."

We headed back the way we entered. Only we were moving much faster and proceeding with extreme caution. The dimness of sunset was approaching. As we high-tailed our way to the rallying point, Renae showed me how to load, unlock and fit the clip into the AR-15. Then she handed it to me. She also inquired about my handgun being loaded as she kept her sleek, camouflage shotgun at the ready. After about twenty minutes we heard gunfire; lots of gunfire from several different weapons.

Renae stopped and looked around. "It's going down," she said. "It's going down! I should've known it wasn't going to be this easy," she sighed.

I could tell by the anxious tone of her voice trouble was headed our way.

And so were the echoes of gunfire. My heart began to pound. Something wicked had been unleashed by the foreign invaders. And we couldn't outrun it. The rest of the team was coming our way with something chasing them. And whatever it was, bullets weren't slowing it down. Judging from all the gunfire, we were in for one hell of a surprise.

Hey, It's Ethan!

"Come on," Renae motioned. "Climb."

It was a tall, sturdy oak tree with one branch just low enough for us to grab onto. It stood at least thirty-feet high with branches and leaves thick enough to hold and hide beneath the cluster of leaves. And that's what we did. I held the AR-15 close to my body. Renae was perched about eight feet away. Her shotgun aimed downward and her finger next to the trigger. Less than thirty-seconds later Roland appeared off in the distance. He was running, shooting, and reloading. Was he shooting at aliens? Was that tall, ugly thing Ray saw outside my window after him? Oh my God! I gulped. We're all about to get probes stuck up our asses. As he got close to the clearing where we were hiding, he began yelling.

"Stay put! I'm trying to lead it away. I love you." He panted like a man running a marathon, still firing his weapon indiscriminately. What was he aiming at? He didn't look scared, just pissed off.

"Who's he talking to?" I asked.

"Me," Renae whispered. I saw her eyes tear up.

"How did he know we were up here?" I asked. He didn't even look in our direction, I thought.

"That's Roland! He's a tracker. He's the best. He knew," she wiped tears from her eyes. I could sense she wanted to respond and call out to him. Perhaps even demand that he climb up here with us and hide. But she remained silent, worried these would be his last words.

"Why didn't he..."

"Shhhh..." Renae gestured to me to be quiet. A great look of concern spread across her face.

A few seconds after Roland ran by, we heard the rustling of leaves, the breaking of branches and the padder of anxious feet. I peeked sideways from an opening in the tree limbs. I had to know what was after him. I stared off into the clearing but saw nothing. Then appearing out of nowhere and seemingly from nothing, a ferocious, scarred up lion was standing there sniffing the air. Its face was distorted into an angry scowl of sorts. Its mane was soaked with fresh blood that dripped from its mouth and whiskers. Its paws looked as if they'd been dipped in some poor guy's guts. It huffed and sniffed the air, checking for the scent of humans...us! There was a huge metallic collar around its neck. It blinked red as it stood still. Then, this fierce beast moved its head in an upward motion causing the collar to blink green and just like that, it disappeared into a clear- to invisible form that began running in the direction Roland had gone.

"What the actual fuck!" I whispered to Renae. "They've got a goddamn invisible lion as a guard dog!"

"It's a light bending cloaking device. Not really invisible," she answered.

"What the hell is the difference? We can't see it," I frowned.

"We've got to get out of here. It's almost dark. We'll be sitting ducks," she whispered. "And don't move. Only shoot when I tell you to." She pointed her finger slightly west. "There are some abandoned buildings about a quarter mile that way. We can buckle down there for the night. And then..." She stopped. Her mouth dropped open. Someone was coming. I heard it too. They were footsteps. Human footsteps. They were talking. They were noisy. They were stupid. It was Ethan. He came towards our hiding place. He had his fancy guns in each hand and his camera attached to a cord around his neck.

"I'm going to blast the fuck out of that thing as soon as I see it!" He boasted to the camera. "By the time you guys see this, I'll be at home drinking a brewski and having that lion mounted on my wall," he laughed.

I wanted to tell Ethan to shut the hell up. But I also wanted to tell him to climb up this tree with us and hide. I looked over at Renae. She signaled for me to be quiet. I didn't know why. Was she formulating a plan? I could tell she wasn't sure which option she wanted to take.

Ethan stood a few feet in front of the tree. He couldn't see us. "Where the fuck is everybody?" He looked around the forest, still fumbling with his phone. I stared over at Renae. My facial expression was telling her to help him. She reluctantly agreed.

"Pssst!" She whispered. He didn't respond. "Pssst!" She signaled again. Ethan looked clumsily around. "There's a lion," she said in a low voice. "Climb up."

"I know," he smiled. "I seen it. And I got these 9mm hollow points for that ass, too." He held up both pistols laughing.

"Just come on!" I interrupted.

"Damn, that you Jack? Is everybody up a tree?" He laughed some more, looking upwards and drawing attention. I don't think he knew the lion was invisible. "Jack, you ain't going to believe this shit, man. I got crazy footage of a spaceship. bro. Before I lost the signal, I was live streaming and..." He stopped and sniffed the air. "What the hell is that smell?" He turned his nose up in disgust.

The smell was the hot, foul breath of savage rage. It was at that second the four canine teeth of the once invisible carnivore appeared along with the rest of its muscular, broad chested body; uncloaked and ready to devour. It was inches away from the kid's face. Our eyes bulged as we stared down at the fate that awaited Ethan.

"Oh shit!" He yelled. The maneater bit down on Ethan's shoulder and neck. Blood squirted out like a water hose that had been run over by lawn mower. The lion dug its teeth into Ethan's shoulder and drug the young man to the ground. It then slapped him with its sharp claws leaving deep gouges in his face. Ethan's blood curdling screams caused my hands to tremble a bit.

"Jack!"...."Jack!" Renae called out.

But I couldn't respond. I was paralyzed by the growls and viciousness of the animal. The lion drug Ethan like an antelope; out into the open, teeth buried deep in his shoulder.

"Jack, God damnit, aim for the head and I'll aim for the body before it turns invisible again," she blurted out.

We climbed down far enough to where we'd be able to jump to the ground. Time was ticking away as Ethan's screams became less intense. I looked over at Renae as I tried to appear brave, while inside, I was terrified. You would think holding on to an automatic weapon would've made me much more solid, but it didn't. Renae nodded and we leaped...together. As soon as my boots touched the ground, I sprayed bullets everywhere. I'd never fired an automatic weapon before, but I felt a surge of power and control. I was still nervous but a lot less afraid. Renae's shot gun sounded like a cannon going off.

"Bloom...bloom....bloom...bloom!" She kept pumping and shooting. We were able to get off at least twenty rounds collectively. The animal leaped backwards, running in the opposite direction. Then it flicked its head back, staring upwards and activating its cloaking device. It's wounded and bloody body disappeared with our fresh bullet holes in its hide. But it wasn't enough to save Ethan.

We ran over to the young man. He was mangled and mauled so badly he was almost unrecognizable. His left eyeball had been clawed out of his head and dangled next to his ear. His shoulder blade was gnawed off and blood soaked the grass around his mutilated body. We stood over him watching his chest struggle to push air in and out of his dying lungs. His right eye blinked as he stared up and into our faces. He couldn't speak because of the tear in his throat. He could only make gurgling sounds. He was trying to communicate. But what did he want to say?

"Goddamn!" I gawked. I'd never seen such a gruesome sight in my life. It made my stomach bubble, and I threw up by his feet. Ethan was trembling as blood pushed its way out of his nose and mouth. I took a deep breath. I looked around and saw his expensive guns lying two feet away from his body. His guns still looked new, and he never fired a single shot. I picked up his camera and phone. Renae looked over at me as if she wanted to say something important but changed her mind. As Ethan's breathing became shallower, his struggle for air became more intense. Renae pulled out her knife and plunged it into his chest.

"What the fuck!" My mouth fell open.

"Run Jack!" She ordered.

"What?" I replied.

"Run Jack! let's go!"

Renae tugged my arm, and we ran briskly towards the abandoned buildings. They were in the opposite direction from where the wounded lion had fled. The first structure we arrived at looked like it could've been an old corner store. The weather-beaten bricks appeared to have a faded logo written next to the dirty, stained window. The raggedy door was unlocked and almost off its hinges. It was unlikely to keep anything from busting in on us. But what choice did we have? We hurried inside and posted up. The one-story building had a picture frame window that had to be covered. Renae checked out the place as I hunched over to catch my breath and calm my stomach.

"Did you see the look on Ethan's face?" I asked.

"Yeah," she said.

"Did you see his goddamn eye hanging out?"

"Of course?"

"Why did you kill him?" I huffed.

"I didn't kill anybody. He was practically dead, Jack. He was suffering. Would you rather have left him there for the lion to circle back around and eat him alive?"

I stared at her. I'd never seen anyone suffer and die or be mauled by a lion for God's sake. Obviously, she had.

"Come on, help me push this cabinet in front of the window," said Renae.

We pushed an old, wooden display case in front of the door as well. We'd found shelter, a safe place for the night and just in time too. The sun had set, and it was officially dark outside. There's no telling what was lurking around those woods at night. And if it wasn't already dead, that wounded lion would be seeking us out for revenge.

The building we were held up in smelled so musty it reminded me of my dad's work shoes. My mother used to make him put his work boots on the back porch before coming into the house. Actually, this three-room structure smelled a lot worse than that. If you added in the standing water and mold, I'm sure it was toxic. As my flashlight reflected off the old, peeling, lead paint, Renae reminded me that our flashlights could still be detected from outside. So, we had to turn them off. I was just glad there wasn't a back door we needed to barricade; one way in-one way out. Although the place was dark and smelly it was secure.

We crouched down in a corner of the room with our guns aimed at the door and waited. The moonlight found its way through the top of the windowpane. In a pitch-black room you'll be surprised how much such a small thing is appreciated. After I'd calmed down some, I pulled out Ethan's video camera and pressed rewind. And there it was, the foreshadowing of his demise. A huge, square, black object hovering weightlessly in the clearing in front of the tallest trees. It was 1/3 the size of a football field, with entry doors, symbols, and markings. It was shaped like a giant square domino with flashing lights and spectrum beams. Ethan's voice could be heard talking shit about how famous he was going to be. Then the door opened up and the lion leaped from inside. It disappeared while he was recording. Then the feed and the recording turned to a fuzzy picture with static. That was probably around the same time I lost my phone signal as well.

Ethan's disfigured face would be stuck in my head, for all time. His last whimpering gurgles would be sounds I'd hear in my dreams, or over coffee in the morning, or in a quiet car, driving home from work. That's how fucked up it was. Who could forget something so dreadful? Who was going to tell the poor guy's parents? Renae looked through Ethan's unlocked phone. He had pretty much the same content as the video camera which means he was doing dual recordings.

"You hang on to the camera and I'll keep the phone. That way if one of us doesn't make it out of here, this video will." After sensing my anxiety, she realized that didn't come out right. She rubbed my leg. "But don't worry, we're both getting out of here, okay."

"Do you think the rest of the guys are still alive?" I asked.

"Jesus Christ, I hope so. What kind of question is that?" Renae sighed.

"What about Roland? That lion was on his ass," I pointed out a painful fact.

"Can't no one lion take down Roland Buntry. Them Buntry boys are hard to kill," she laughed. "And Roland is the toughest son-of-a-bitch I know."

"Can I ask you something?" I mumbled.

"What?" She sighed.

"How long you two been married?"

"Seven-years. And before you ask, yeah, we're kind of separated, okay. We still live under the same roof, but I guess the seven-year-itch has us both kind of doing our own thing now. But that doesn't mean we don't love each other. It means, that if I choose to make you my boy toy, I can," she chuckled.

I smiled. "Boy toy," I mumbled. That wouldn't be so bad considering how hot she was. I wondered what she looked like outside of hiking gear and Rambo boots.

"But I wouldn't tell Roland. He's a psycho when he gets jealous," she warned.

"No shit," I mumbled.

"Anyway, I'm going to take the first watch. You get some sleep," she ordered.

"I don't think I'll ever be able to sleep again," I yawned. I was too nervous to close my eyes. The room was so damp, dirty and fucked up I didn't want to lay my head against anything. But the thought of something possibly knocking down that door and attacking us wasn't going to allow me one second to relax.

Renae reached through the darkness and squeezed my face. She moved in close and kissed me softly. "Maybe this will help you relax," she kissed me some more, rubbing her cheek against mines, brushing her soft lips over my eyes and brows. She even poked her tongue into my ear, which immediately woke up **Stiff John**. She rubbed her hand across my zipper to see if I had an erection. "No!" she whispered. "We're not going there. I just wanted to replace your fear with something a bit more... calming."

Even in the darkness I could see her teasing smile. "Okay," I gulped.

"I'll wake you up when it's your turn," she said.

Her relaxation technique worked. Instead of falling asleep scared, I fell asleep horny.

A few hours later it was my turn to take watch. Renae settled in a corner of the room to rest. It was eerily quiet outside. But then again, it was quiet from day one. I was actually kind of glad. It meant nothing was going on. I couldn't help but wonder what happened to the rest of the team, if they were dead or alive. Or maybe one of them got back to the vehicles and went to get help. Then again, they didn't seem like the kind of guys who would go get help. They were the help. I also wondered if any of them came across Ethan's mangled body? I could still hear the excitement in his voice when he told us about the video footage. Maybe if he'd listened more...maybe if he weren't so hardheaded...maybe...

I stood up to stretch my legs. The numbness from sitting on the hard floor gave me muscle spasms in my thighs. I had to walk it out. I went over to the window and peeked through the section that wasn't covered by the dusty cabinet. The moon was bright, clear, and yellow. It reminded me of a giant flashlight glowing in the sky, creating the shadows that emanated from the trees. But there was something else. Something was in motion. Something that wasn't a shadow nor was it my imagination. A tall, thin figure moved as if it floated above the ground. It went from tree to tree, peeking, looking, and hiding, headed in our direction. Although I couldn't see it clearly, it looked like the alien creature Ray described outside my window.

"Pssst, Renae!" I whispered. "Renae, wake up!"

"What is it, Jack?" She mumbled.

"Come look out this window. It's those aliens. They're... trying to... sneak up on us," I stuttered. My palms began to sweat.

Renae hurried to the window.

"Look through that section of trees to the right," I instructed.

"Fuck!" She exclaimed. "There's something standing there, watching us. And it damn sure ain't human."

"Put your respirator on," she whispered as she tightened the clamps of her own worn-out respirator around her ears.

A few seconds later a deep, booming voice echoed through the trees. *Help....help ... Oh God, somebody help.* It was her husband, Roland.

"Goddamn, they got him!" I shook my head.

Help me... please... Renae... somebody! He screamed like a man in pain; a man being badly tortured.

Renae stood quietly. She didn't budge. But I looked out the window again and the alien with the ugly face was gone. And now it was just Roland; down on his knees, beneath the moonlight, waving his arms for help.

I can't walk. My knee is busted. Help! He belted out curse words. *God damnit, somebody help me. It's all right! It's safe!*

"Come on. Are we going to get him or what?" I asked.

Renae chuckled. "Those alien assholes have to do better than that."

"They're gone. It's just him over there crawling around," I answered.

"That's not him," she stared solemnly out of the window.

"What are you talking about? We have to at least try to help him," I replied.

Renae squinted as she stared unblinkingly through the dirty, glass pane, listening to her husband's voice become more desperate. "Do you listen to rap?"

"What," I asked.

"Do you listen to rap music, Jack?" She repeated.

"Some," I answered.

"Well in 2012 I went to the Coachella Valley Music Festival in California."

"Renae, what are you talking about? Concerts... rap?" Clearly, she was becoming unbalanced from the pressure.

"Just listen, Jack," she said. "And right there in the middle of the concert Tupac appeared on stage and started to rap."

"Wait, you said 2012? 2Pac died in 96," I recalled.

"Exactly!"

"Oh shit! I heard about that. It was a hologram. It was all over the internet. First of his kind, they said."

"Yep!"

"So, you're saying that's not really Roland, but a hologram?" I asked.

"That's right. These things got at least a thousand-year head start on us," she sighed.

"But what if you're wrong?" I countered. I was in no hurry to go out there, but I knew he'd do it for me.

"There is no circumstance in the world where Roland Buntry would lure a comrade out into the open, more or less his wife. But they wouldn't know that," she smiled.

"Jesus Christ, these aliens are Goddamn diabolical, " I shook my head. Shouts for help went on for at least another half hour. And then it stopped just as suddenly as it began. No one was out there, nothing but dead silence again. Renae and I sat side by side about twenty feet away from the door. Our guns were locked and loaded.

We were ready to put down anything that came through that archway. My blood was pumping faster now because I knew they weren't finished. They wanted us contained. They needed us silenced. But we were determined to live.

"How come they don't just blast through the door or blow up the building?" I asked.

"They don't want to leave evidence, Jack. They want their presence here to remain secret, ambiguous, and lure. They want the rest of the world to laugh whenever they hear someone say they were abducted by aliens," explained Renae.

"We got to get back to the city and expose these bastards," I sighed.

"I figure we've got less than an hour until sunrise. Then we're going to hightail it the fuck out of here," said Renae.

After a while, the sun rose and so did my spirits. I began to feel a bit more optimistic; like in a few hours I could actually be at home in my living room, downing a tall glass of liquor, with my hand down my pants scratching my balls. That picture in my head made me laugh. And I needed a laugh. But right in the middle of my pleasant thoughts of surviving this nightmare, a deep, resonant voice interrupted my projected happy ending.

"I knew you were different. I knew you weren't going to fall for the usual screaming hostage routine."

I peeked out of the window. No one was there.

"We're going to have so much fun, you and I, Jack."

I grabbed my head. It was pounding. From my temple to the back of my neck, throbbed. What the hell! It was happening again. A voice in my head; interrupting, sinister, antagonizing. It had been well over a month since that Persian cat had me questioning my sanity. Now there was another voice. It was more frightening and gave me an instant migraine.

"Your team has been scattered to the wind and soon their remains being picked over by turkey vultures," it laughed arrogantly.

Renae moved in front of me and looked out of the window. "You've got a new friend I see."

"Wait, you hear it too?" I asked.

"Of course, I hear it. That's the voice I heard last night. But right now, it's giving me a serious fucking migraine."

"Yeah, it gets worse," I mumbled.

"So, how is this possible? Who is this talking?" She asked.

"The aliens experimenting on animals. They gave them the ability to use telepathy. They can communicate with humans within their proximity without ever opening their mouths," I explained.

"Well Goddamn!" Exclaimed Renae, shaking her head. "What's the point to that?"

"I don't know," I shrugged. "Probably just for their amusement."

"You said you were communicating with a Persian cat?"

"Yeah," I answered.

"Well, how did it get out here?" She asked.

"The cat that was communicating with me is dead."

"So, what's this in my head?" She asked.

I took a deep breath. I knew we were in trouble, big trouble! "This is something else. Something big, angry, vicious, and blood-thirsty. More likely, the lion that killed Ethan," I replied.

"I'm sure we hit that son-of-a-bitch multiple times. It should be dead," she said.

As the light from the sun seeped through the cracks and corners of the window, and from beneath the raggedy door, I could see the disappointed look on Renae's face.

There was something out there waiting for us. "Maybe it's not the same one. I don't know. But what I do know from experience is that they're extremely aggressive and fearless," I answered.

"You got any more good news?" She asked sarcastically.

"I could have eaten you last night. It took a lot of restraint not to gorge myself with your liver and intestines. I saw you standing around your little fires, looking up at the moon, admiring its glow. That Moon isn't real. You're a species of fools. That's the glow of a spaceship from a dead civilization filled with the dried-up bones of your ancestors."

Renae and I both looked at each other in surprise. It was a mind-blowing revelation. But would we live to tell anyone?

"Get ready, Jack. I think it's going to try and bust in here on us," warned Renae.

"I'm ready!" I replied, planting my back firmly against the deteriorating wall. My hands were trembling. I squeezed the nozzle of my AR-15 so that she couldn't see how scared I was. Renae stood on the opposite side of the door with her shotgun fully loaded. We wanted to catch the beast in a crossfire. That way one of us would be sure to get him. We waited anxiously. Ten minutes turned into twenty, and twenty into forty. But there was silence, and nothing happened. I kept staring outside through the small opening in the dusty blinds, careful not to move them too much and alert anyone to our presence. After an hour, I felt relieved.

"What do you think happened," I asked softly.

Renae had her game face on. She was ready. She didn't answer. It was as if she was hypnotized- staring at the door, on the verge of pulling the trigger. Maybe the lion had found someone else to hunt, trap and kill. I felt kind of bad for thinking that, but I was glad it wasn't us.

It had to be at least 10:30 or 11:00am in the morning. There were still no birds, or crickets, or sounds that you'd normally hear in the morning. But now, I understood why I hadn't seen a deer, or rabbit, or snake, or turtle... nothing. The Grays had run them off. Evicted them from their own forest. That's when I saw movement off in the distance. Someone was walking towards our building; headed directly for our hideout.

"Someone's coming?" I squinted.

Renae hurried over and took a peek. "It's Matt." She looked a bit disappointed. I could tell she was hoping it was Roland.

"Matt, the tech guy," I remembered.

Renae slowly nodded as if she was trying to digest what was going on. Then came a huge smile. "Goddamn, he's wearing thermals. That smart son of a bitch," we both laughed. An invisible animal would be easy to see wearing those.

Matt was a lean, nerdy guy who had a skinny body with a big head. We could see right away he was wearing heat signature visors. They reminded me of 3-D glasses you'd wear in a movie theatre. But thermals could detect the presence of anything with heat in its body, even during daylight.

"Come on, help me push this cabinet out of the way," said Renae.

I was again feeling optimistic. Someone else besides us was alive.

"Over here!" I waved my hand cautiously. Matt dashed towards us with the reckless abandonment of a schoolboy chasing the ice cream truck. He had a big grin on his face. I thought for sure the lion was going to get him.

"Thank God!" He sighed. "I was starting to think I was the only one left." He stepped inside and slid the glasses into his pocket.

"So did we," I replied.

"You didn't see Roland or Quinn?" Asked Renae.

"Not since the lion jumped out of that spaceship. You should've seen it! It was magnificent," he explained.

"What, the lion?" I asked.

"No, I've seen plenty of lions. The spaceship. It's almost half the size of a football field, with lights and doors and..."

"I know. We watched Ethan's video," I sighed.

"You did?" Exclaimed Matt.

I held up Ethan's camera.

"Well good. Poor kid. I saw what was left of him back there. And it wasn't pretty. Geez, hell of a way to go," Matt sighed, criss-crossing his chest like a Catholic Priest. "So, what's the next move? It's only about a twenty- mile hike out of here. Ten hours give or take."

"It's going to be less than that if we run halfway," said Renae.

I noticed Matt's clothes were soaking wet, and they clung to his skinny body. "How'd you get so wet?" I asked.

"I spent the night hiding down an old water well. I had my trusty thermals, but I didn't want to take a chance on traveling at night by myself, so I climbed down and went to sleep," he answered.

"Good thinking," said Renae. "We've got a better chance of getting the hell out of here with three of us. You got any more of those glasses?" She asked.

"I do not. But don't worry, I can see well enough for all of us," said Matt.

"Did you see anything on the way in?" I asked.

"No, everything was quiet and clear," he answered. "Although I do think we should leave now and make a run for it. In fact,"

Suddenly, the floorboards begin to vibrate.

"Is this an earthquake?" I asked naively.

"Worse," Renae answered.

"What's worse than..." Before I could finish, the wall in the next room began to buckle. The old ceiling tiles fell to the floor along with hundred- year-old dust and asbestos. Sheetrock busted wide open as a huge crack the size of a doorway appeared on the wall. Something was ramming the exterior wall so hard the small wooden building shook. What the hell is going on?

"Get ready, lock and load," frowned Renae.

Did she know what was happening?

As the cracks in the wall got wider, daylight began to beam through the opening. Ready or not something awful was coming for us. A deep, bone chilling growl emanated from the other side of the wall. Then a pair of red, beastly eyes quickly peaked through the hole then backed away. It definitely wasn't that lion, which meant the lion was still out there; still hunting us. Possibly waiting to ambush us right outside this door. Whatever kind of creature that could break through an exterior wall was not to be fucked with. Once again, we moved the cabinet from in front of the door and waited.

"When it bursts through the wall, that's when we run," said Renae.

Matt and I looked at her and nodded. We were both too afraid to utter a word. I knew Matt was scared because his hands shook worse than mine. After all, he was just the tech guy. Fighting villains or battling other world creatures was not in his job description. On the way here, he told me he graduated at the top of his computer science class at Columbia University. About ten years ago he started his own computer software company but got voted out as president during a hostile takeover. He figured that if we found alien technology in these woods, he could leverage the new innovations to get his company back. But now, here he was holding an automatic weapon, fighting for his life, and praying he'd make it back home like the rest of us.

There was more rumbling. The ground shook as whatever this thing was, ran towards the building again. "Bam!" What was left of the wall instantly crumbled and fell apart. Wood, dust, and debris blew into the room as particles filled the air making it hard to see or even breathe. Rays of sunlight poured in along with a huge, four-legged beast that reminded me of a giant aardvark without a snout.

"What the fuck?" I yelled, as we all started shooting. But the creature lowered its large head like a charging bull. Our bullets bounced off a bulletproof, metallic object that covered its head and the majority of its massive body. We ducked and coward from our own ricocheting rounds.

"Awe, goddammnit!" Matt grabbed his knee and fell backwards; shot by his own deflected bullet.

"Let's go!" Renae yelled. She yanked open the door, ready for whatever was waiting on the other side.

I put my arm around Matt's waist, and he hopped on one leg as fast as he could. But he didn't get far. The wrinkled, grey colored, creature's teeth locked onto his ankle and snatched him back inside. I grabbed his wrist and pulled as hard as I could. Then I heard the creature's teeth clamp down even harder on Matt's leg. The bones in his ankle crackled like a car tire over broken glass. I was now in a life and death tug-of-war to save the tech guy's life. His face was etched in fear as he clung to my wrist for dear life. But the beast was much too powerful.

Matt's outstretched arms looked frail protruding from his inspector gadget coat. His eyes were filled with water and desperation. I was no match for this dominant beast and Matt was unknowingly pulling me back inside the building with him, dragging me to certain death. But he wouldn't release my arm. I braced my foot against the rickety doorway and continued to pull backwards.

"Let me go!" I screamed franticly. I saw the red glow of the creature's eyes and knew how evil and relentless it was. But Matt had that 'I don't want to die alone' look in his eyes and refused to let go of my arm. I had to do something, so I bit down on his hand as hard as I could. Matt stared into my eyes then lowered his head as if to acknowledge his moment of shame and weakness. He pulled his thermal imaging glasses from his pocket, then let go.

I watched in horror through the archway just beyond reach of sunlight, as Matt was dragged kicking and screaming to his doom. All I could see was the creature's wicked, red eyes glance up at me in between biting and devouring it's screaming victim. I didn't want to bite that man but there was no need in both of us getting killed.

"Come on Jack. We can't help him," Renae yelled. "We've got to split up. One of us has to make it back with these videos or he died for nothing."

"Wait!" I said and picked up his cracked thermal glasses off the ground.

"Go that way about two miles, turn left, and in five more miles you'll see the interstate. Good luck!" She nodded hastily, flashing a quick grin of reassurance, then ran off.

Maybe I should've given her the glasses or at least offered them. I ran as fast as I could, pumping air in and out of my chest, trying to pace myself like my high school gym coach taught me. It's funny what the mind thinks about in moments of great stress. After coach Jenning's face popped up, I thought about my next high School reunion. And if I'd make it out of these damn woods to get there. I thought about kissing Apryl Winston during a Friday night football game. It was my first kiss. I also tried to finger her and got head-butted. It was my first head-butt as well. I was running, sweating, and scared; scared to stop moving because if I did something could catch up with me. I had watched another man die a horrible death. Another man who's screams I'd have to hear the rest of my life; however long that would be. And once again I was helpless to do anything about it. So far, it was aliens two, humans zero.

Running For My Life

I'd never been in the woods by myself. Sure, my dad took me hunting sometimes but my experience with nature came from outings with my boy scout troop 262 in Evesham Township, New Jersey. We mostly slept in sleeping bags, learned how to tie knots, rubbed sticks together and played fart games- tag you're it. But now I was alone. And in survival mode. Time was running out. It was too early to think about sunset and darkness. But I could tell it was late afternoon. I had to keep moving. Although my run had dwindled down to a sprint and now a jog, I refused to stop moving.

I must have covered at least three miles non-stop. My ribs were aching. I was coughing and spitting up phlegm. I was out of shape. My adrenaline had kept me going or maybe it was my fear. But now, my chest was hurting it was time to rest. I had to stop. I leaned desperately against a tree, hunched over like somebody's old grandpa. I was wheezing, coughing, and feeling like I was about to pass out. But at least I was alive. I was here. And I intended to stay that way. After about ten minutes I was beginning to feel better. I had caught my breath and was ready to push out my second wind. I took two steps forward and fell down. Not because I was clumsy, but because there were two gnawed up dead bodies blocking my path. What the hell? I jumped and looked. Their necks had been ripped open and their chest, face, and clothes exhibited lacerations and claw marks.

It was obvious the lion had devoured two more poor souls. I looked hastily in every direction, determined I wasn't going to be next on its list. But the leaves in the brush behind me begin to crackle. Oh my god! I turned around in haste expecting to see teeth and claws. Instead, a warm, dirty hand covered my mouth and pulled me to the ground.

"Shhhh!" The voice whispered. His long, funky fingers under my nose almost made me sneeze and gag at the same time.

"It's watching us!" The man said as he wrapped me in a camouflage blanket disguised as grass and leaves. He dragged me into a small, shallow grave he'd dug in the earth.

It was Preacher. The one arm Captain Ahab who'd been searching for his alien white whale for years.

"Jesus Christ, dude, I could've shot you," I gulped.

"Trust me, you're not that good, kid," he smirked. "Look over there. You should've seen him as soon as you walked up- with those glasses on."

I looked about half a mile through the trees, and barely visible, dug halfway into the earth was that lion. It was cloaked, but it's red outline was almost unnoticeable. Even with my thermal glasses on, I may not have seen it until it was too late. I was sure as hell headed in that direction.

"He's a sly son of a bitch. Patient too," said Preacher.

"You think it knows we can see him," I asked.

"Hard to say. But I'm guessing, yeah. It's picking its time of attack, carefully. Or maybe its job is not to attack us but to protect the ship. It can smell us all the way over there you know."

The way preacher smelled; I wasn't surprised. "Thanks," I sighed. "I would've walked right into him."

"Right into his teeth," replied Preacher. "Where did you get those glasses. I thought me and Matt were the only ones who had them?"

I didn't have the heart to tell him that his associate Matt was dead. "He hurt his leg. He said I could use these to get help," I lied.

"Good. But he's going to miss all the fun," smiled Preacher.

"And what did you mean when you said the lion was protecting the ship?" I asked.

"Well, after we kill that lying-in-wait S.O.B., we're going in there," he pointed about 150 yards away from the lion.

"Goddamn! You mean I missed that too?" My mouth dropped open. I couldn't believe my eyes. It was the alien spacecraft that Ethan had recorded.

"Breathtaking, huh?" Asked Preacher.

It looked even bigger now because it was live, in color, and in my face. It was black and shiny with dim lights all around. Hidden by the trees, it hovered about 5 feet off the ground. I could see the splotchy red die the airplane had dropped on it. It reminded me of a Navy battleship, ready, intimidating, and sophisticated. Right in the middle of me gawking at, and admiring this phenomenal craft, I realized what preacher had just said.

"We're going in?" I asked with trepidation.

"Of course. We're going to kill those son-of-a-bitches," he lowered his glasses, and I could see his eyes. They were unusually big; like he was coked up or something. Or maybe he had gone crazy.

"I.... I...I... I don't think that's such a good idea," I frowned. There was no way I was going into that goddamn spaceship. That would be like breaking into somebody's house while they were home. And that never works out. After we kill that lion, I planned on running as fast as I could in the opposite direction. But I wasn't about to tell this one arm vigilante that his holy alien quest for revenge wasn't going to include me.

"Don't worry kid. I've got a plan." The old man opened up his jacket and showed me five hand grenades hanging from clips on a hunting vest.

"Holy shit!" I blurted out as I tried to stand up. I'd only seen hand grenades in movies. But now I was lying next to a guy with about half a dozen pinned to his body. I didn't know if I should run and take my chances with the lion or wait for this guy to sneeze and blow us both up.

He pulled me back down. "They're safe kid. You have to hold and pull before they go off." He chuckled after seeing how scared I was.

"Roland said we weren't going to engage them. We're supposed to just get the evidence and leave," I frowned.

"You think I came all this way for a few shitty pictures that the government and NASA will tell people was a hoax? Hell no! I plan on dragging one of them ugly, grey bastards through town square. Or at the very least, chop off an arm. An arm for an arm, how's that!" He laughed and patted me on the shoulder.

Preacher's thermal glasses were the same as mine, dark, wide, and dorky looking, so I couldn't see his eyes this time. But did I really need to? This guy was on a suicide mission. He was just like that captain in Moby Dick; chasing that whale and getting everybody killed. Now, I was glad my 11th grade teacher made us read that book out loud in class. Yep, I was going to haul ass in the other direction as soon as we killed that lion. My entire attitude was in survival mode; get to safety, get back home. And yes, I was full of regret. I wished I never watched that goddamn YouTube video. And I sure as hell wished I never walked into these goddamn woods.

I was getting increasingly nervous as the sun began to set. Time was moving fast. Darkness was approaching. What tricks would those fiendish aliens have for us tonight? We were out in the open, in a small hole with nothing but a blanket covering us. My eyes were hurting from wearing those infrared glasses for so long. But I was too afraid to take them off.

"How long have you been waiting here?" I asked.

"All night long," said Preacher. One of those lions walked right past me too," he said.

"Wait, you mean that lion over there wasn't the only one?"

"No, I waited longer than everybody else before I left. I saw at least three lions and something else come out of that ship," replied Preacher.

"Damn! I'm glad I didn't know that earlier. I thought that was the one we shot."

"It's not," he frowned. "So that was you who put lead in the one I found dead half-a-mile that way?"

"Me and Renae," I nodded.

Preacher smiled. "Good work, young man." He gave me a fist bump.

"But doesn't that leave two?" I asked.

"I'm not sure. Could be more. But Roland killed one with his titanium, double edge, hunting knife. You should've seen it, man. The goddamn thing was invisible, but it was attacking his brother, Quinn. So, he couldn't use his gun right, because if he did, one of those bullets would've torn right through him. So that crazy fucker ran, leaped into the air, and came down pushing that knife right through the top of the big cat's head. It was like watching a god-damn action movie."

"Wow!" Roland was a real badass alright. I wished it was him under this smelly blanket instead of preacher. I didn't have anything against the guy, but he was on a suicide mission. I also wished I wasn't laying in this wet spot. It hadn't rained and Preacher had been hiding here all night. That meant I was probably lying in his piss. Oh my God I want to go home!

I couldn't help but wonder why the aliens inside that massive, technological power station didn't zap us with a ray gun like they did in the movies. They had the technology. What was holding them back? What was keeping them subdued? I guess such an outburst of energy would alert everyone to their presence. It could be picked up on satellites. It's always seemed The Grays primary objective was to remain unidentified.

Just before dark and just before I was about to take those annoying, migraine causing, heat signature visor things off my face, I saw a familiar form walking boldly through the woods. He was cautious and watchful yet appeared to be unafraid. Did he know what was out there? Did he know there was a bloodthirsty animal lying in wait, protecting that spacecraft like a rabid guard dog?

"That's Roland!" Exclaimed preacher. "It's Roland!"

I tilted my glasses and peered from beneath the camouflage blanket. It was indeed Roland; knife in one hand, Desert Eagle .44 Magnum in the other. The red silhouette of the lion began to move and wiggle. After sitting still, dormant for hours, it stood up, shook, and stretched like felines before a hunt. And now, it seemed our fearless leader Roland was his intended prey.

"Roland can't see that lion, we got to help him," I said hysterically.

"Oh hell!" Preacher huffed. "On three, stand up and start shooting at it, short bursts. Make it come towards us. At least we can see it. Here," he handed me an extra clip. We both had the same identical AR-15's. "When it comes, move over by that tree. We're going to catch it in a crossfire. And kid, try not to shoot me, okay," he said.

I was nervous. These lions were smarter, faster, bigger, and stronger than the average lion. And after seeing what happened to Ethan up close, I was even more reluctant. But we had two things poor Ethan didn't; thermal imaging glasses and fully loaded, combat, assault rifles.

"One... Two... Three...!"

We both rose up like SEAL team six veterans, guns blazing. Fire and smoke poured from our weapons. I let out five rounds, then waited a few seconds and let off five more. Preacher did the same. Even from over 60 yards away, through the trees, I could see the look of surprise on Roland's face. He knew we were helping him. Although the lion was cloaked, Roland pointed his gun in the direction we were firing and let off a few shots of his own. He then dropped to one knee and waited, both gun and knife extended head tilted to one side, listening for what he could not see. But we could see the Lions large, red silhouette full of muscle and stealth. Our barrage of bullets dissuaded the animal's attack. It ran off leaking from the holes we put into its body.

I pulled my glasses off and hurried towards Roland like a child rushing to Santa. I was glad to see him, happy to see he was still alive. It removed some of my anxiety. The guy knew what he was doing. He was a professional. He was the guy in charge. Once again, hope jumped back into my mind along with steak dinners, vodka and orange juice, and the possibility of sleeping in my own bed tonight.

"Roland, you made it," I smiled."

"Easy kid. Good to see you, too. But put those glasses back on," he ordered.

I complied, then looked around. The coast was clear.

Preacher walked up. "Roland, I see you're still with us."

"Yeah, shit really hit the fan this time." He looked over his shoulder at the ship, looming near the tree line. "They're probably watching us right now."

"So, let's go say hi," said Preacher.

"We're not here for that. It's time to get the hell out of here. Have you seen the others? Where's Renae? Quinn went to find y'all and didn't come back."

I shrugged like I didn't know. I didn't want to tell him what happened.

"Look, this is our chance to strike one for the home team," said Preacher. "Maybe even send those bastards straight to hell."

"The only bastards that'll be going to hell is us. Have you been paying attention to what's been going on out here? Now stand down!" Ordered Roland. He folded his arms. "Or will I have to subdue you for your own safety?"

Preacher smiled and removed his thermal glasses so that we could see his eyes. He handed them to me; sweaty and fogged up. "This ain't my first dance with these aliens. They think they're so goddamn clever. But I can't think of a time since my first encounter, they haven't haunted me. I can't stop thinking about them; all day, most days, since they took my arm. And any connection I had to friends, neighbors, family, or anybody who gave a damn about me, has been long gone. The world just moved on without me and I've been stuck in this goddamn nightmare. I don't want to wake up screaming no more. I don't want people to call me 'that crazy old man with one arm,' no more." A grim look appeared on his face. His eyes were watery. "I'm done. That's it! I mean, how can a man go back to being normal after experiencing what I have; what we all have? Ten years ago, my life went to shit, man. My wife left me. My daughter hasn't spoken to me in over ten years. My best friend was abducted by these assholes. I lost my arm. I lost my pension. And I almost lost my damn mind." He bit down on his lip anxiously. "I'm an old man that's tired of being alone," he said calmly staring over at the spacecraft. "I ain't got nothing left. And I ain't got nothing to go back to. Ain't nobody gone miss me. That means you don't get to decide for me, Mr. hero, how the Preacher chooses to meet his maker." He looked at Roland with the most solemn expression I'd ever seen on a man's face. I immediately knew where this was headed. I also knew I wouldn't see him again.

"Here," he handed Roland his AR-15. Then handed me a grenade. "Stick that in your shirt, under your armpit, kid. You'll know when to use it," he winked. "This was one hell of a mission, huh chief?" He smiled at Roland. The men gave each other affirmative nods. Then the old man turned and began walking. He passed the trees and headed into the open field towards the spacecraft. He never looked back.

Roland glanced at me and sighed. The big man was emotionally powerless to change Preacher's mind. He knew Preacher wasn't going to stand down. And tussling with him amidst all the danger we were in was a bad idea. Roland also knew he had no right to decide when, where or how a man was to make his last stand. And no matter how much it bothered him, he had to let it be.

"Who is that I smell? Is that you, Jack?" The deep, gargled voice in our heads made Roland and I grab our ears.

"Oh shit!" I gulped, as the hair on the back of my neck stood up.

Roland instantly pivoted and looked around, gun at the ready. "Who the fuck said that?" He asked. "Why does it feel like it's in my head?"

"That... that creature, man. It's using telepathy," I frowned. In all the excitement I'd forgotten it was still out there, stalking and waiting.

"Telepathy?" Repeated Roland.

"Those aliens, man. They did something to these animals. They're all fucked up, experiments and shit. They're bigger, faster, smarter and bloodthirsty as hell. And they can communicate with humans if they choose, using some kind of telekinesis," I explained.

"You got to be shitting me!"

"No sir, I shit you not," I replied.

"Where is it at?" asked Roland, looking through the trees.

"I don't know I squinted. I figure they can communicate with us from at least a quarter mile," I said. "And this creature has on some kind of bullet resistant armor. The bullets just bounce off and go everywhere."

He took off his thermal glasses and stared at me. "You're full of good news. Is there anything else you need to tell me kid?" He frowned.

I hesitated. "It's the same animal that attacked the building me, Renae, and Matt were held up in."

"Is Renae..."

"No, I mean... I don't know. We got separated. But Matt; he didn't make it." I shook my head. "That thing grabbed him and..."

Despite how big and tuff he was, I could see Roland was relieved to know his wife could still be alive. Obviously, strength was no match for love. "First off, never withhold information from your team. It could mean life or death."

I nodded. He was right.

"Second, we're still alive and we're in deep shit, stay focused."

Preacher was now running towards the vessel like a man who didn't have a care in the world. He was less than sixty- feet away and all we could do is watch. We were rooting for him. Although we had no idea what his plan was. His mind was made up and he was resigned to his fate. The enemy ship hovered about five feet off the ground and without his other arm preacher seemed to be at a bit of a disadvantage. But climbing was the least of his concerns.

"There are three of those cloaked lions closing in on his position. It's like someone wrong a goddamn dinner bell," said Roland.

Where in the hell did they come from? They were ignoring us because their primary goal was to protect the alien spaceship. And Preacher's mad dash towards the vessel was the immediate threat. We were supposed to be gone. We weren't supposed to be going any-where near that spacecraft. But I knew Roland wasn't about to leave Preacher to be eaten alive like some sacrificial lamb, no matter how self-destructive he'd become. Roland moved in closer to get a clear shot. I watched him pause, hold his breath, then squeeze the trigger.

It was a head shot and one of the lions instantly fell. Then, he moved forward about five- feet and with short bursts, took down a second one. The third lion moved in a zig-zag pattern; unpredictable and cunning.

"Shit, I can't get him!" The third lion was moving too fast. Roland stood up and tried waving to preacher; to warn him. But it was like the one arm man had blinders on and refused to look back.

Preacher got his outstretched hand onto the ship. He quickly lifted himself up like a man doing one arm pull-ups. He stood on top of a narrow catwalk in front of a triangular opening. Was that a doorway of some kind? The cloaked lion leaped easily onto the two-foot-wide walkway and crept slowly towards our determined team-mate. Its cloaking device was now deactivated allowing Preacher to see the fate that awaited him. The oversized, menacing animal walked slowly towards him, taking its time, and savoring the prey it was about to devour. Preacher didn't seem afraid. He was calmer than I ever could've been. He backed up against the oddly shaped entryway and held his arm above his head. We could see there was a grenade in his hand. I now knew what his plan was.

"Can you shoot that last one?" I asked. Still hoping to save Preacher.

"Negative, one of the bullets could hit him or those grenades, then what?" Said Roland.

Right there in the midst of Preacher's last hurrah, the ghastly beast that had been tracking us and fucking with our heads, decided to make its presence known. The thing that had torn Matt's insides apart, had walked up behind us. Its red eyes captivated me, like a hypnotist's watch. I was paralyzed with fear and all I could do was stare.

Even with the hair on the back of my neck at full attention, I was somehow able to tap Roland on the shoulder. He immediately turned and began firing. His onslaught of bullets flew everywhere, ricocheting into trees and at times barely missing our heads. Then the creature began barreling towards us, charging like a raging bull.

"Time to die!" Echoed in our heads.

"Run!" said Roland.

The big, lumbering creature was fast for its size. It pivoted around trees and within seconds was chasing us through the open field towards the spaceship. I could hear it snarling as it gained ground. The closer it got, the more noise it made. Its growl was deep, frightening and resounding.

As we ran from certain death, our eyes were on Preacher. We watched helplessly as the lion leaped onto him; mouth open, seven-inch teeth extended and claws tearing at the man's chest. Preacher's face was etched with an evil grin as he stuck his entire arm holding the grenade into the cat's open mouth. The oversized lion then tried to rip his shoulder from the socket.

"Shit! Get down, Jack! Cover your head and ears." Roland yelled.

"Boooooom!"

The grenade exploded inside the lion's stomach and caused the other grenades Preacher was wearing to detonate as well. The enormous explosion shook the ground. It felt like I was in the bumper cars at an amusement park and continuously getting rammed. My ears and eyes watered immediately. Blood, skin, and animal parts littered the ground ahead of us as blood rained onto our faces.

The fiery glow overtook the sunset. Smoke billowed from the hole that was ripped into the side of the alien craft. And to our great relief, the charging animal retreated because of the noise. It seemed disoriented, annoyed, and confused. A few seconds later something that reminded me of steam sprayed out over the fire. The smoking flames turned into particles and fell to the ground.

"We can't fight this thing in the open and at night, " said Roland. He looked at me, then at the hole that was punched in the side of the ship. "Well, let's go!"

We climbed up and onto the edge of the spacecraft. It was cold and didn't feel like any metal or steel I'd ever touched. It felt like an old Pepsi can you'd take to a recycling plant. My hands and feet also touched a mushy substance. Although I tried not to think about it, I knew it was probably Preacher's guts and brains I was walking in. it was unavoidable. Although I felt bad for him, I had to acknowledge how brave the guy was. He went out like a real soldier. The team captain and I stood in front of the hole the grenades had made. We looked back at the large beast that was pursuing us. It danced around in the shadows of the open field. It couldn't seem to get itself together.

It appeared that our deceased Captain Ahab was going to have his way after all. We were about to walk inside an alien spaceship, an actual UFO, and engage with probable, hostile extraterrestrials. And if we lived to talk about it, it would be the greatest story ever told.

Into the Mouth of Death

When we stepped inside the lights came on automatically. They were fluorescent and bright. There were no bulbs, switches, or out-lets. I expected to see cold iron walls with bodies hanging, alien goop, and pod clones. But there were none. I thought I'd smell foul, monstrous odors and be overwhelmed by otherworld stench. But there was no smell either. At least nothing that our human noses could detect. In fact, the ship was just as clean and accommodating as a hospital maternity ward. It was like a sterilized museum; nothing out of place.

We put names and titles on our doors. They used pictures. There were color coded entryways, and the equivalent of LED screens the size of doorways. They automatically began to display moving pictures in

3-D, so life-like and real you'd want to reach out and touch them. Each archway showed images of star systems, planets, and technology. It was like watching the live stream of other planets and their inhabitants; strange creatures, playing in a pre-recorded loop. There were birds no human had ever seen before. Some beautiful and exotic. Others, ugly and frightening. I saw plants, trees in the middle of the ocean, rivers that were red and sand doons the color of rainbows. There were huge animals that could fly and reptiles that looked identical to earth's prehistoric dinosaurs.

"What does that look like to you?" Roland asked as we passed the doorway with familiar images. I stepped towards the hologram, prompting the door to automatically slide open. We both stepped cautiously inside. There were about twenty tanks with large, hairy creatures encased in what looked like cold steam. They weren't dead but they weren't alive either. They were frozen in place. Their eyes were open and staring at nothing.

"It's those damn bigfoots people claim they see," I frowned. "So, they're not even from this planet," I mumbled. I had a feeling a lot of things were never from this planet. They were brought and released here, stuck here, or escaped here. I realized, things that go bump in the night aren't always our imaginations. But instead, something truly out to get us.

"Let's go," said Roland.

As we continued down the winding corridor, we glanced in amazement at what I called previews, that began to pop up. Now, these large, colorful archways displayed the brief history, final encounter and abduction of other world inhabitants. Some were hideous creatures, plucked from their natural environments, or homes. Others were tiny and fragile, and made me wonder what possible use The Grays had for them at all. That's when I came across another surprise, although it shouldn't have been a surprise.

There were pictures, stills, and clips of an American family. I could tell by their car, clothes and buildings, they were old. These images looked like vintage home movies someone had colorized. They were recorded decades ago. There was a man, his wife and two children: a boy and a girl. They were having a fun afternoon on a secluded beach, cooking out, playing, laughing, and happy. Then, just before sunset, something appeared on the beach in front of them. It crawled out of the water, a deformed, hideous thing, and right up to the mother. The woman was horrified. She screamed. The husband hurried towards her and was instantly caught up in some kind of beam that made him unable to speak or move. His face looked twisted and tormented. He trembled like a man having a seizure. The two children tried to run but were sucked up into the air and disappeared in the low-lying clouds. Whatever was recording the video placed a yellowish marking on the parent's foreheads before they too were sucked up into the sky.

Roland and I stared at each other in disgust. We had to go inside. When the sliding door opened, we immediately noticed the room was colder than the other one. We also saw fluorescent operating tables, digital charts with indecipherable writing, monitors, and life-sized tubes that resembled upright coffins. There were at least forty of those. And of course, the first tube we came across contained the father we'd seen in the video. He was encased in green liquid, and we could see his heart, veins and organs beating on a monitor connected to the glass. His face was angry, brows and mouth curled into a frown with tense jaws and lips. His eyes were closed, and he was naked. I'd surmise he knew what the aliens were doing to his family, and he hated them. His wife was in the tube next to him. She looked sad. Her sullen face was as long as a violin. Her eyes were puffy from crying. Their children were incased in tubes across from them and still had toys in their hands. They were all frozen in time, trapped a few feet from one another but would never kiss or hug each other again.

"Goddamn, this is fucked up," I sighed. Roland could only look over at me. I know he was thinking the exact same thing. An entire family was abducted. Their lives inexplicably cut short. Frozen in some puke, green substance to be thawed out and used like meat you'd keep in your deep freezer. Down from them was a woman with a 1920's hairstyle. Across from her was a scarred up, bearded man who could've walked straight out of a Charles Dickens novel. So many people have inexplicably gone missing. Entire families with people who loved and needed them. Never to be seen again. And here they were. These aliens have been abducting humans for years, dissecting and experimenting on us. Throwing away the parts they didn't need. They had no conscience. No empathy. No fear.

"Come on, there's nothing we can do for them," said Roland. Interrupting my bitter thoughts of fury and revenge. When we walked into the hallway a sharp pain hit my forehead, then that deep, horrifying voice began to speak.

"Oh Jack, I hope you and your buddy Roland are enjoying the sights. You're the only two who ever made it this far."

"Did you hear..."

Roland nodded his head 'yes' and put his finger to his mouth signaling for me to be quiet. He'd heard it too, alright. And we knew the animal had made its way back onto the ship and was nearby. We hastened our steps. But steps to where? Where were we going? Did our mission change from evidence gathering to seek and destroy? We eventually found ourselves in the middle of a large room. It was octagon shaped with no furnishings. As humans, we were used to rooms filled with stuff; tables, chairs, carpet, pictures, mirrors, decorations, and clutter we needed to show off. But these aliens only had the essentials. However, there was a hologram of one of The Grays playing in a loop. It was wearing some kind of headdress and insignia. It must have been someone important. It was the first time I'd seen one. And it was ghastly.

It was tall, maybe 6' 4" to 6' 5" with a thin, dusty, gray body that was slightly hunched over as if it had severe scoliosis. The eyes were like the buttons off a Navy sailor's uniform; round and shiny. Its mouth was but a slit and it had no nose; at least not in terms of how we view a nose. There was a thin cloth covering its body. It extended down to where it's dick was supposed to be. It made me wonder if these aliens took a crap the same way we did.

"This is as good a place as any," said Roland.

"To do what?" I asked.

"To take down the beast that's been stalking us," he answered. "In here, it can't build up momentum enough to charge us and we can find a vulnerable spot in his armor."

The encounter I had with the four-legged beast ended badly for the gadgets guy, Matt, and forced Renae and me to separate. God knows what was going to happen now. I could only pray I didn't end up like Matt.

"All armor has a connecting point, find it and shoot. Short bursts. Aim for the eyes, neck, legs, and feet. At the very least, we can shoot them suckers right out from under him," said Roland.

We stood on each side of the entry way, guns at the ready. I'd seen this animal in action, and I was fucking terrified. I felt like my bladder was about to explode and I'd just pee all over the creature instead of shooting it. Roland noticed my fear or just my face changing colors and tried to help.

"Easy kid. Take deep breaths. You want to get back home to your family, right?"

I nodded.

"Well, this is what it'll take." He pulled out his long hunting knife and put it in his mouth.

That's when an immense feeling of dread poured over my body. I became extremely anxious. My hands started trembling. I felt trepidation and panic. Was I really that scared? I was breathing faster. My heart, pumping. I stared down at my hands shaking uncontrollably like I had Parkinson's disease. Then my AR-15 dropped from my fingers and fell by my feet. I tried to pick it up, but I couldn't control my muscles. I couldn't move. I looked up at Roland. There was a blank expression on his face. He was also shaking; his gun and knife had fallen by his feet.

What the fuck? He had been hoisted into the air, levitating like the girl in 'The Exorcist' movie. Holy shit! I looked down; I had also unknowingly been lifted off the floor. This wasn't fear or anxiety we were experiencing. It was them. It was the aliens. They were here.

What entered the room was no hologram. Nor was it the beast that had been taunting us. It was the invader. One of The Grays. It had taken control of our bodies and removed our weapons. The thing that came into the room had a big, bald, hairless head. Its shiny round eyes were so wide I could see myself in them. It pressed the button on its belt removing a red field that encased its body. That must have been some type of force field. It moved towards me, gliding like it had on roller skates. I was petrified and stuck like a fly caught in a spider's web. It reached out its arm and I could see its hand was comprised of four, long, wrinkled fingers that were mashed on the end. Why did it come towards me first?

The alien grabbed my face like it was inspecting fruit at a farmer's market. I knew it was angry. We were on their ship. We'd come to kill them and expose them to the world. Then, like Ray told me he'd seen that night on my balcony, it's slither of a mouth opened up the length of a whiskey bottle. It exposed rows of long, sharp teeth, like a walking piranha. A thick liquid that can only be described as saliva dripped from its anticipating tongue. This meat eater was about to take a bite out of me. This was it! This is where my journey ends. My great adventure was at its conclusion; defeated by the goddamn aliens.

"Fuck you!' I yelled. My eyes filled with water. I stared across the room at Roland. He squirmed and wiggled trying to break free of the invisible force that locked us into place. I could see the disappointment in his eyes for being unable to protect me.

"Hey, you bastard! it's me you want. Leave the kid alone," he yelled frantically across the room.

"They were supposed to be my treat, master." The voice echoed throughout the chamber. It made the alien close its mouth and step aside. I could see the shadow of the large beast looming in the hallway. "You fools entered the secret hall of the Reticulans. This is a shrine for the greatest of all their kind. That is his likeness you see in the moving picture. Oh the pain you will suffer for such a violation!"

The alien moved further out of the way to allow the beast to take me. It was as if they flipped a coin to the see which of them would eat me alive. In those last seconds I thought about my mom and dad. How they'd miss me. And if I'd been a good son. They, or no one else, would ever find out how or why I disappeared from the face of the earth. I thought about some of the beautiful women I'd been with, Ray's bar, and what I was going to miss. I wished I had more time to spend with Jen. I was going to make her my girl when I got out of this mess. Did I have regret? Sure, I wished I never came to Connecticut. Hell, I wished I had never rescued that damn cat in the first place. I wished I could've stayed blindly in The Matrix where I was safe.

The alien's favorite beast walked in like it owned the place. "What the fuck is that?" Asked Roland. He'd never seen it close-up.

"I am your worst nightmare. Your horror movie come to life."

The four-legged beast walked towards me, saliva dripping from its canines. Now, I could see it clearly. The thing that ate Matt. The thing that would eat me. It was about eight feet long and weighed at least a thousand pounds. The parts of its body that weren't covered with bullet resistant armor, looked dark gray, wrinkled, and deformed. The menacing creature stopped in front of me, stood up on its two hind legs and growled like nothing anyone had ever heard. Its breath was like a blow dryer against my face and neck, and smelled like a dead cat you'd pass by in a field. My stomach immediately erupted causing me to puke all over myself. But puke wasn't the only thing that came out. My staring such a horrible death in the face caused immediate streams of urine to run down my pants leg.

I looked over at Roland. His eyes were bulging as he helplessly watched my impending death unfold. I closed my eyes, anticipating those yellow, shiny teeth on my neck. Then I heard something fall to the floor. I opened my eyes back up to see the menacing creature had ripped the control belt and garment off of its master and was chasing him. The exposed alien moved wildly throughout the room with its own pet in deadly pursuit. The fleeing Reticulan circled back towards me trying to get its control belt but reached down and instead, hit a button that freed me and Roland from our paralysis.

I hit the floor. My adrenaline pumping. I was alive. I was almost dead but now I'm alive! I immediately grabbed the grenade preacher gave me, pulled the pin, tossed it at both of those sons of bitches, and hit the floor. The explosion didn't do what I expected but the animal and its alien master both let our blood curdling howls. They were both discombobulated. Lights started to flash and flicker. Steam began to shoot out from everywhere. Yet in the midst of it all, I could see that the huge animal still found its way back over to its master and had cornered the alien.

"Oh master, how could your highly intelligent brain, that I will soon be eating, not see this day coming? I will no longer be your slave." The immense animal had penned the skinny alien to the floor. Its thin arms flailing about. Then the beast bit its scrawny neck, pulling it away from its body like chicken gristle. I stared in disbelief. But I was also cheering for all the people these things had abducted. It was a fitting end. Destroyed by its own monstrous creation.

"Let's go!" Roland yelled.

We ran desperately back in the direction we came.

"Sorry, I didn't hit much with that grenade," I told Roland.

"You did good, kid. Real good," he gave me a fist bump.

It only took us a minute to get to the hole we came in through.

"Leaving so soon, Jack?" That animal's voice shocked my insides like fingernails on a chalk board. "He was the last one. The other Recticulans got careless around a bunch of young lions and ended up their main course." It laughed sadistically. "You were a great distraction. Instead of chewing off your face, maybe I should thank you. Again, there was deep laughter.

We climbed onto the ledge of the craft. The ship had lifted another 8 or 10 ft into the air. And to top it off, a light rain had begun to fall making the exterior of the object slippery and dangerous.

There was an ominous breeze blowing through the forest. The trees waved as their limbs moved with the wind.

"Well kid, no one's going to bring us a ladder," Roland huffed. "When you hit the ground lean forward and roll."

Lean Forward? What the fuck! We were almost three stories in the air. I shook my head. The spaceship was tilting back and forth. But the beast was coming. I could hear the patter of its huge feet running through the hallway. It had made quick work of its master. And its deadly rampage was going to continue with us.

"On three," said Roland. "1...2...3..."

We leaped into the darkness, feet first, fear second and not a moment too soon. I saw the red eyes of the other world beast as it took a swipe at me from the blown-out hole. Its huge black claws barely missing my face.

As soon as my feet touched the grass, I sprung forward and rolled trying to lessen the impact. But it didn't matter much. I heard bones cracking, both mine and Roland's.

"Aww!" I yelled. My arm and leg felt like they'd been hit with a hammer.

Roland winced in pain. "I think I dislocated my Goddamn shoulder," he said holding his left arm.

More noises and lights came from the alien ship. A loud humming sound was followed by dozens of pops that reminded me of 4th-of-July firecrackers.

"You humans are consumers. You go through everything like locust. You hunt and kill and take pictures of it. You eat for fun and take pictures of it. Tell me Jack, who's going to take pictures of me eating you?" I could see its red eyes staring down at us from the spaceship. But would it jump?

"Can you walk at all?" Asked Roland.

"I cracked my knee and elbow."

"We need to get out of here. That thing seems to have a hard-on for you, buddy," said Roland.

"I know," I sighed. When I tried to stand up my knee wouldn't let me. But Roland was able to get to his feet. He reached over and practically lifted me up by my shirt.

"Suck it up! Let's go! Let's go!" He ordered.

The rain began to fall more steadily now. And in some strange way it felt good. We were still alive, still fighting to survive. More crackling and popping sounds came from the spacecraft. As I hobbled on one leg, I looked back at the spaceship now gently rocking back and forth like a child's swing set. Was it about to explode? Suddenly, the loud growling and snarling of the beast filled the air. "B-o-o-m!" The ground shook.

The huge, sadistic beast had jumped from its dead master's spaceship. It was free to roam. Free to hunt. Free to destroy. And the first thing on its list was me. We were scrambling, moving as fast as we could, but my knee gave out, causing us both to fall into piles of wet grass and muddy leaves. The vicious beast moved quickly; its red eyes looked like two lasers charging towards us in the darkness.

"We can't fight this thing out here in the open like this," said Roland. "I don't have a gun or knife. Not even a goddamn tree limb," he coughed trying to catch his breath. He held his dislocated shoulder and grinded his teeth in anger. He had dragged me and my busted knee for almost sixty yards, but I could tell he didn't have anything left in him. Roland was hunched over, panting, searching the dark forest ground for a weapon. But there was none. And just like that, the bloodthirsty animal was upon us. We both crawled backwards on our hands and feet while watching this vicious beast slowly stalk us.

"This is so fucked up!" I said frantically, staring into the beast's red eyes. They were just like the Persian cats; frightening and wicked.

"Any last words, Jack?" The voice echoed in my head.

The vicious creature stood up on its hind legs, poised to attack, ready to bring all its weight down upon our injured bodies. It was showing its dominance and invoking the ultimate fear in its prey. Its claws, molars, inserts, and canines shined in the moonlight as it prepared to bury its teeth in my flesh. And there I was again, bracing myself, body tensed up ready for the impact of this other world monster's fatal aggression. Then suddenly, the creature's head exploded like a pinata at a child's birthday party. Blood squirted out of its torso as its remains oozed all over my legs.

"What the hell!" Roland's mouth dropped open like a broken mailbox. He lowered his head in great relief.

I laid there for a few seconds with the animal's blood and brains running down my face. I was in shock, staring up at the moon. The rain from the skies as well as rain drops from the trees dripped on my head. I was happy to feel them. I even opened my mouth to let some water drip down my dry throat.

"Did its head explode," I asked, finally able to speak.

"That thing wasn't wearing a collar. The impact wasn't from a bomb," said Roland. "Oh shit!" He grabbed me again and began dragging me as fast as he could.

When I looked up, the disabled spacecraft was falling to the ground, breaking through the trees and headed towards us. Once again, Roland had guided me to safety just in time. There was a loud explosion, sparking fires among the fallen trees. A tidal wave of dirt splashed all around us, followed by debris, branches, rocks and dust flying everywhere. The once intimidating vessel now looked like a grounded boat that had gotten stuck in shallow water. And soon it would be explored by the same humans the Grays appeared to despise.

Roland propped me up under a tree and we both sat there and laughed; happy, maybe even surprised to be alive. Less than five minutes later someone was shining a flashlight in our faces.

"Goddamn, did you see that shot, son? Did you see that shot? Half a mile... in the dark... in the rain!" The voice was awfully familiar.

It was Ray, dressed in fatigues, wearing black and green camouflage makeup, carrying a gun almost as tall as him.

"Who the fuck are you?" Roland scrambled to his feet.

"That's my buddy Ray," I smiled. I was overcome with joy. I hugged him like I was hugging life itself. My eyes filled with water.

"Well, great shot marine!" Roland hunched over a bit but still managed to extend his hand.

"Ray shook his hand with a smile. "How'd you know I was a Marine?" He asked.

"Because only a fellow Marine could make a shot like that. Rytec sniper rifle with armor-piercing, explosive bullets."

Ray nodded. "Sergeant first-class John Raymond Williams at your service," he saluted.

"How did you find us?" I asked, wiping the dirt, mud, and hysteria off my face.

"When your phone signal went out yesterday, I knew shit was about to hit the fan. You weren't hard to track."

"Yeah, shit hit the fan and was blowing everywhere," I sighed.

"I would've been here sooner, but you guys had men down in the field," Ray sighed.

"Who?" Roland squinted.

"Curly head guy who said he'd been mauled by a couple of lions. He's missing a finger and maybe an eye, but he'll make it," replied Ray.

"My brother Quinn," Roland sighed in relief.

"And a woman. She fell into a man trap. A spike went right through her leg, too. Once I stopped the bleeding, I pulled her out of the hole. Shit, she was ready to come back this way."

It was easy to see Roland was relieved. A smile appeared on his face. And it was the first time I saw him smile since we met.

"I had to promise her I'd help you guys before she agreed to go with the park rangers," said Ray.

"That's my Renae alright," he smirked.

"It appears you sir, saved me and my family. I'm in your debt. And I thought I was the baddest motherfucker in Connecticut."

"Well, we're sharing that title today. Let's get the hell out of here." Ray looked over at the remains of the beast covered in dirt and had been pushed up against broken trees by the fallen vessel. "Who the hell shaves all the hair off of a female bear?"

Roland and I looked at each other. Then hobbled over and stared at the animal. Ray was right. We couldn't see it at the time. This was no other world creature. No beast from beyond. But instead, another earthly mammal The Grays had turned into their guard dog and killing machine.

"Gentlemen, I don't think we should hang around here in case your alien friends got other alien friends who may be looking for them. I've got a four-wheeler about half a mile that way, let's move," said Ray.

On the way Roland saw the bloody caucus of one of the dead lions and borrowed Ray's hunting knife. He savagely cut the head off and held it up in the air.

"Jesus... dude, you're taking a souvenir home?" I asked.

Roland smiled sneakily and pulled the invisibility collar from its severed neck. The aliens had trained them to use it to their advantage against us. Now Roland was going to use it to his advantage. "Fucking aliens!" he mumbled.

We hobbled, limped, and carried each other through the woods. Everything from my toe to my tailbone ached like hell. But I limped my way to Ray's four-wheeler and half-an- hour later, out of Dark Entry Forrest forever. I was busted up pretty good, but I was alive. I was in one piece. I survived when so many others didn't. To say this was a life-changing experience would be a gross understatement. I'd walked blindly into the unknown; some may say foolishly. I was literally in the lion's den because we underestimated our enemy. Why were these aliens so merciless and evil? Then again, why would aliens treat us humanely when they're not human? How can we expect a far advanced group of beings to view us as anything other than lab rats; especially after seeing the way we treat each other.

I still had so many questions. But at least I knew what to look for and what to expect from these invaders. Maybe someday I'd find the courage to write a book about the adventure of a lifetime and wait for the backlash and ridicule from non-believers and skeptics. But for those of you like me, who've seen stuff and been through stuff, well, we're in an exclusive club aren't we? And membership could cost you your life!

I felt kind of bad climbing into Rays spotless truck with so much dirt and filth all over my hair, face and clothes. I knew how particular he was. He looked at me and smiled.

"Relax, I'll send you the cleaning bill tomorrow," he said. Then he started laughing.

"What?" I asked. "I know I look like shit."

"It's not that," he sighed. "When you first told me a cat was talking to you, me and my old lady started calling you Dr. Doolittle behind your back. And in light of recent events, I'd like to apologize for that," he laughed harder.

"Oh, that's so fucked up!" I laughed along with him, causing my ribs to hurt. "Thanks for saving my ass. I thought I was gone, man." A lump appeared in my throat. "If you hadn't ..."

"Forget it. You would've done the same for me. Except you probably would've shot me instead of the bear. You hardheaded motherfucker!"

"Here it comes," I mumbled.

"I told you so! I told you not to go, didn't I?" He shrugged. "I knew some crazy shit was gone happen, running off into the dam woods. But noooooo..."

All I could do was smile, nod and listen to his 'I told you so', all the way down the road. He was right.

As we sped along the interstate, my weak, dehydrated body slumped down on the passenger side of Ray's SUV. I looked over at the hotel my car was parked at. I was in no condition to drive. "I'm going to get my car towed back to New York tomorrow, so just keep going. But I do want to make one stop on the way home."

"What, the emergency room?" Asked Ray.

"Yeah, I'm going to the hospital." Then I held up Ethan's video camera. "But first, stop by The New York Times. I've got one hell of a story to tell them."

- The End-

Julius Kane is a busineman who resides in the DMV Area. He is the author of the sci-fi series **Bone Snathers From Beyond The Realm.** Julius Kane is the author of the popular novella **Alternative To Divorce** as well as the suspense drama **Innocence Denied: Forced To Play The Game.**